PROLOGUE

THURSDAY
1 OCTOBER 2015, 10:42 A.M.

MINA KNEW JACK WAS PRESENT, but not here. He was a layer away from her reality. She could almost feel his hand in hers, like the first sensation of an itch that just couldn't be reached. One of her fears was that the itch would disappear completely before she had a chance to scratch it. Her overriding fear at the moment was being captured or killed before she could make contact with him. The main library in San Francisco was vast and open to the public; six floors, nearly 400,000 books, plenty of corners to have an inconspicuous rendezvous. And it was quiet. One scream or loud noise and the whole library would know something was happening. Everyone would be on alert. The streets outside were almost always busy. Plenty of witnesses.

For the first attempt at contacting Jack, Mina had picked another public setting, Pier 39 at lunch time, from intersection list she and McKenzie left him to find. The loud barking of the sea lions would have been lost in the winds off the bay or blended in with a scream had the situation warranted it. Mina aborted that meeting when she saw Cochran's henchman eating chowder at a restaurant near the entrance of the pier at an outdoor table. It was a bright day and unusually warm for San Francisco in late September. His back was to Mina as he studied the crowd, but she recognized him from a previous incident when he threatened her in Wyoming, the day before McKenzie disappeared or died. Mina was there to make contact with Jack at the Carousel near the end of the pier. Jack had taken her there on their first date about two years ago. It seemed like twenty years ago. In retrospect, the Carousel was possibly the worst place to go. It was surrounded by shops and restaurants, and there was only one way in and out of the pier. She had learned from that mistake. She had become a lot wiser over the past few weeks. 'Sadder, but wiser as the Coleridge poem expresses,' Mina thought to herself.

'How had they known where she was planning to connect with Jack?' Mina wondered for the hundredth time. 'Are they here now, in the library? What have I missed? Is this a dangerous location too?' Mina walked in the door, glad to be out of the bitter wind that always seemed to converge on the corner of Market and Hyde. She had spent the last two hours in a seat at Burger King across the street from the library's side entrance, watching everyone going in and out. She hadn't seen anyone to raise her concerns. Of course, there was the main entrance into the library around the corner on Larkin, but this was the less conspicuous side door, and she could only watch one part of the massive building. The library felt warm and safe. Jack and Mina had used the library as a meeting place while they were dating. Mina was an IT expert who had worked as a software programmer at Twitter Headquarters just a block away. Jack was a Supply Chain Manager, located at a nondescript office deeper into the Tenderloin District. The library was a perfect place to hold hands and talk before they both caught the BART to go their separate ways; Jack to his apartment in Berkley and Mina to Millbrae where she would trade the BART for her 2010 Honda

Fit and drive home to Santa Clara. In those days five million people were in between Jack's place and Mina's. Today they lived in two separate universes with literally billions of people and the laws of nature in between them. If things went as planned today, for a moment, they would be the only people in their own combined universe.

Mina wasn't sure what a security expert would do at this point. Should she walk around the library to see if she saw anything suspicious so she could safely abort her meeting again, or would that just alert anyone looking for her where she was? Maybe she should go directly to the meeting location as quickly and directly as possible, limiting the amount of time others could spot her. She decided for the middle ground, to walk indirectly to the set meeting point. She could at least see if anyone was following her without attracting any attention. It would be easy to act natural, like someone looking for a book, to double back and look around. She eventually made her way to the Corner Reading Room on Level 4 with three minutes to spare.

As she had guessed, the room was empty. No one had appeared to follow her. As she sat down in the chair on the left side of the table, she pulled the handwritten note from her pocket and placed it in her right hand, palm up resting exactly at the center edge of the table. She placed her left hand, palm down, just an inch from touching the table with the left side of her hand touching the light stand connected to the table, exactly three feet from hand to hand. She had practiced this at McKenzie's place until her hands and arms ached. She hoped the muscle memory was still there. She stared directly ahead, willing herself not to blink and thinking of Jack, the love of her life. Thirty seconds later her hands twitched. The note in her right hand disappeared, and in her left hand she squeezed the note she had retrieved. She closed her eyes and searched her near-term memory. There he was, Jack, smiling at her. He had dark circles under his brown eyes, and he had a three or four-day beard. But it was Jack, she was sure of that. She sat there for another minute, knowing he was in the seat right across from her, looking at the empty seat across from him, where she sat. Tears welled in her eyes, and despite the success of the moment, she began to weep quietly. She wrapped her arms around herself and bowed her head.

"Are you alright?" a voice at the door asked.

Mina looked up and saw a stooped old man with wispy white hair and a cane through her tears. "I'm fine," Mina said. "Just missing someone really bad."

"At my age, I know that feeling," the man said. "But you are so young. You need to live the life that is waiting for you just outside the library doors."

"My life was just sitting in that chair," Mina said, nodding to the chair across from her before she could stop herself.

"Oh, I see," the man said. "I lost the love of my life just a month after we both retired. We had so many plans. Five months after her passing I was sitting on a park bench, just up the street from here. Do you know the Yerba Buena Gardens? I was a curator at the Museum of Modern Art across the street. Before I retired I would eat my lunch in the park, weather permitting. Sorry," he said realizing he was wandering off the topic. "As I sat there wishing for what life had taken from me, the clouds blew inland and the sun hit me with such force that it woke me up. You see, I was so inside myself, I didn't even realize how cold I was. The warmth felt so good. I was amazed that with all the sun had to worry about, at that moment, it delivered welcome rays to my tired body. I have not looked back since. This is another one of those kind of days. Go outside and let the sun to its job." Before Mina could reply he continued his stroll to another part of the library.

"He's right Mina," she told herself. "I have a note in my left hand that is from my best friend, and I need to enjoy it out in the sunlight." She got up, but before she left the room, she blew a kiss to the empty chair. As she turned back around to exit the room, she bumped into another man. At first, Mina worried it was the old man and that she would knock him over. This person, however, was a young oak tree. As she mumbled an apology and moved away from him, she could feel the solid muscles in his arms and the scent of eucalyptus on his skin.

"I am so sorry miss," this younger man said. "I wasn't expecting anyone in the reading room. I would guess it is not usually a social place."

"That's why I come here sometimes," Mina said. "It's all yours now." She saw the concern on his handsome face. His blue eyes were smiling, but the rest of his tanned face showed concern. He looked familiar in a distant way. Was it his cleft chin that reminded her of somebody? He was handsome. He moved his eyes away from her like he was uncomfortable or had said something wrong. Maybe he had used this place back when she frequented the room just last year.

"It's none of my business," the man said, "but are you okay? You've been crying."

"Oh, it's nothing," Mina said. "Just an emotional day. Thanks for asking though."

As she turned to leave again, she saw Cochran's closed shaved shiny head looking over the railing to the ground floor center area. Mina turned and touched the man's arm, as he was slowly heading off in the other direction. "Excuse me," Mina said. "Could you do me a huge favor?"

"I suppose," the man said turning back to her. "What can I do for you?"

"Could you escort me to the lobby?" Mina asked, hoping she wouldn't have to explain.

"Uhm, sure," the man said. "Any problem? Mina took a big breath and let it out. "That man over there seems to be following me. I saw him earlier. He just keeps popping up where ever I'm at," Mina said. "He gives me the creeps."

The young man studied Cochran for a brief moment and said, "Yeah, he gives me the creeps too. There is something a little strange about him. Looks like he's on drugs or something. Wait, you're not pushing or buying, or, I mean, tangled up with some gang or something that's going to get me in trouble, are you?"

"Nothing like that," Mina said.

He shrugged his shoulders and said, "Okay, let's go."

They walked down the hallway with Mina praying Cochran didn't look her way. He must have caught their movement in his peripheral vision because just as they walked past him, only four feet away, he spun around and recognized her. "Hello Mina," he said, paying no attention to the young man.

Mina pretended she didn't hear him and as relaxed as she could pretend to be, she grabbed the young man's arm and said, "Are all FBI Special Agents as strong as you?"

Mina could feel the young man tense up, but to his credit, he didn't say anything but kept walking. Neither looked back but kept walking. Their timing was perfect and jumped on the elevator with another young couple. The door closed before Cochran could join them. Mina thought, perhaps he hadn't planned to take the elevator. Quickly Mina pushed the button for the second floor.

"I thought you wanted to get out of the building?" the young man asked her.

"I do, but not with that weirdo following me," Mina said. "Is there another way out of here?"

The other girl in the elevator looked at her boyfriend, then poked him. "Ouch," the guy said.

"I am sorry to listen in on your conversation," the girl said. "Andrew works here. He might have an idea, right Andrew?"

"Umm, right," Andrew said. He gave his girlfriend a smirk and pulled out an ID card. He held it up to a small metal square just above the floor buttons, and the elevator beeped. When the door opened on the second floor, he said, "Just wait a second." The door closed and Andrew touched the floor 5 button. "I can override the floor selections," he explained. "Sometimes we need to move rare books or other objects of value using these elevators. As a precaution, we can override the interior and exterior request buttons. Let's get out on the 5th floor."

They all quietly stood there staring at the elevator doors. On the 5th floor, Andrew stepped out first, followed by the young man Mina had commandeered and who by now was fidgeting, obviously wondering what he had gotten himself into. The two young women stepped out together. Andrew led them down a hallway to an unmarked door. He again used his library ID card to electronically unlock the door, and they all passed through. Andrew ensured the door was shut behind them and then walked past several offices to another elevator.

"This is a freight elevator the employees' use," Andrew's girlfriend said. "Andrew uses it for his bike."

"We move a lot of books, art, and furniture with these elevators," Andrew said. He pushed the first-floor button.

They all got out on the first floor and Andrew escorted them to another nondescript metal door. He opened it and said, "This will take you to the employee parking lot and the back entrance.

"Thank you all so much," Mina said as she shook each person's hand like they had just rescued her from the sinking Titanic and staring at the young man she had first commandeered to help her. Somewhere she had seen that square jaw before. She ran to the back entrance, peeked through the fence to make sure it was safe to leave and then walked out the gate and caught a taxi. Slumping down in the seat, she tried to plot her next move. Then she remembered the note in her pocket. It warmed her hand as she felt its crinkle through her slacks. She couldn't wait to get back to her hotel room.

Minutes later she opened the door to her room at the Hotel Triton. She chose this hotel because the manager was an old friend from her Twitter days. She had cashed out her stock options and bought a part ownership in this boutique hotel halfway between Union Square and China Town, with the Financial District to the East and Nob Hill to the West. She hadn't contacted any family or other friends and didn't want to use her credit cards in case they could be traced. She was alone, afraid, and unsure of what to do next. Hopefully, this letter from Jack would give her a clue.

Cochran exited the library and motioned to Paxton who was standing across the street watching the main entrance. He knew something had just happened and he had missed it. 'Who was this FBI Agent? Some family friend? No, she was talking to him like she was getting acquainted.' He stopped his internal conversation when Paxton reached him.

"Where is she at?" Paxton asked.

"Cool your jets, Pax," Cochran said. "She pulled in her own protection, and I had to back off. She has to come out sooner or later. We'll follow her from a distance to see where she is living."

"And we know her next meeting spot," Paxton said, spitting on the sidewalk and getting frowns and disgust from the passersby.

The supposed FBI Agent left the library wondering if he should try to catch up with Mina. He saw Cochran and Paxton talking across the street. He ducked back into the library and left from the side entrance. He had done his part. It was time to go home.

CHAPTER 1
JACK

MONDAY
14 SEPTEMBER 2015, 6:37 A.M.

"I will be RIGHT BACK," MINA said. "I just want to get a bottle of water and some gum to help me stay awake. You want anything?"

"Yeah, get me a bottle of water too, and a bag of Cheetos," Jack said. He watched Mina walk into the gas station convenience store. Even the view of her back took his breath away. Her long dark hair and olive skin were hints of her Armenian heritage on her father's side. Her petite boned body hid her Dutch and Danish heritage on her mother's side. While Jack filled the gas tank, his mind wandered to the previous day's events. He and Mina were on their first road trip together. Their first move together. Since their marriage seven months ago they had experienced a lot of firsts together. First apartment together, first love, first vacation together, first married couple disagreements, first awkward silence, first realization it would take much more to stay together than either had imagined. But their relationship was stronger than it had ever been and they were ready to take on these new changes.

"Mina to Jack, the tank is full," Mina said pulling him out of his thoughts. "All systems go for permission to reenter earth's atmosphere."

Jack pulled the nozzle out of the gas tank opening and inserted it back in its holder. He replaced the tank cap before speaking. "Thanks, Mina," Jack began. "I was just thinking about our firsts. I suppose I am just getting tired, but my mind didn't want to shift back to the present. You got my Cheetos, right?"

"Yes, I got your precious Cheetos," Mina said smiling. "Firsts, huh. I thought you said you were getting tired." Mina leaned against the car in an attempt at a sexy pose. She knew that wasn't her forte and that she probably only looked silly. She loved this Cheetos obsessed man and he made her feel special, but she still worried about looking silly.

Jack grabbed her and held her tight. He gave her a long kiss while secretly trying to reach for the bag of snacks Mina held in her left hand. Her body felt good and he brushed away her dark brown hair from her face and looked into her hazel eyes. "You know I probably first fell in love with you because you have these tiny orange flecks in your eyes that look just like Cheetos."

Mina punched him in the stomach playfully and pulled the snack bag away from his clutches. She ran around to the passenger door of their 1987 Saab 900. "I am going back into use the restroom, which I should have visited before buying the food. It's filthy, and there was nowhere to set the bag. If you are good and don't eat all the snacks before I get back, I will give you a special prize." She tossed the bag through the passenger window and returned to the store.

Jack again watched her walk away, considering whether to follow her just to be closer, or to attack the snacks. Since the windows were down and it would take too long to roll them up and lock the car, he decided to stay with the car. He jumped in the car to find the Cheetos. He no sooner than found the bag, that he felt childish and a little guilty. He had this odd feeling come over him. If that bathroom was so terrible, maybe he had better accompany her into the store. He jumped out of the car and ran to the door in time to open it for her.

"I decided I'd better use the restroom too," he said to a surprised Mina.

"You go first then," Mina said. "I might take a few minutes. I will check out the fishing guides I noticed, for my cousin."

Jack shrugged his shoulders and went into the bathroom.

* * *

He exited the bathroom and didn't see Mina, but remembered he had forgotten to lock the car so he left, figuring she would see him walking to the car. He waited by the car for five minutes and then eight minutes, looking for Mina to exit the store. Fearing she might be sick, he went back to the store. He walked to the restrooms, and no one was in line, so he knocked on the women's room. No answer. "Mina, it's Jack. You okay?" No answer. He tried the door, and it was unlocked. He knocked again and called her name. He slowly opened the door, his heart beginning to beat faster. "Mina?" he said once again, to an empty bathroom.

Jack turned and hurriedly looked around the store. A middle aged woman was looking at selections in the candy aisle and a man, probably her husband, grabbing some water bottles. They had pulled up to the gas station while Jack was waiting for Mina. He turned to the attendant behind the counter and asked, "Did you see a young lady, twenty-five years old, shoulder length brunette hair walk in here a few minutes ago?"

"I haven't seen any young women in over an hour," the man at the counter said. "Believe me, I would've noticed. This is the most boring part of the day."

Jack wanted to yell that she had been in here twice and the first time she bought some things, but he didn't. "Is there another exit, a back door?" Jack asked starting to panic.

"There is a delivery entrance, but I don't use it. That door has been padlocked for years. It's hard enough to secure the front doors," the man explained.

Mind if I check it?" Jack asked.

The man was about to say no but saw the anxiety in Jack's face. "Go ahead, but if you take more than fifteen seconds, I am coming back looking for you."

Jack ran to the back door and tried it. It was locked like it hadn't been opened in years. The padlock even had a spider web on it. He looked around the back room, but no Mina anywhere. Jack walked back out to the front of the store and walked down the three junk food aisles in case Mina had slipped and fallen, hitting her head, and was lying unconscious. Not sure whether to be glad or sad in proving that possibility wrong, Jack walked outside. 'Maybe she had walked outside when I was turned to the gas pump, and she was back at the car waiting for me to unlock it' Jack suggested to himself.

"What the..?" Jack said out loud. The car was gone. "Is this some kind of joke? Where is the camera?" He actually looked around and on the roof to see if there was a security camera. He found it and walked inside to talk with the cashier.

"Could I view your outside security camera? Either my wife has taken the car as a joke, or it has been stolen," Jack asked.

"My camera only goes a few feet out the door, but you are welcome to look at it, the guy at the counter said. "It only holds a digital recording of about two hours in length and then starts recording over itself."

"That is enough time," Jack said. He watched Mina come in the store and then nearly forty-five minutes later he saw himself come in the store and then go out. He was dumbfounded. He walked around the back of the gas station and back to the front. The back door had not been opened. Three oil drums were sitting by the back door that someone would have to climb over to get out the door and there was a half inch of dust and grime on the barrels. There was no way someone could have climbed over them without making a mark.

Jack walked back inside and didn't even ask permission to go to the back of the store one more time. He rechecked both bathrooms again and behind the counter. "I need to make a phone call," he told the cashier. "My car was just stolen, and my wife is missing. My cell phone was in the car."

"Are you sure your wife didn't take the car?" the cashier asked with a chuckle. "You wouldn't be the first to get dumped at this gas station. Well, maybe you are the first," he said trying to stifle his laugh.

Jack continued to look at the clerk speechless. "Okay, you can make a 911 call. I don't want to be stuck with you all day," he said.

The police arrived twenty minutes later. They found Jack sitting on the curb in the parking lot. "Are you Mr. Gamble, Jack Gamble?" the officer asked.

"Yes, that is me," Jack said with hope in his eyes. He stood and approached the officer.

"You reported your car stolen?" the officer asked to confirm.

"Yes, I think so. About half an hour ago," Jack said. "My wife is also missing."

"So, your wife was in the car?" the officer asked.

"No, at least I don't think so," Jack explained. I was filling the car with gas and my wife, Mina, went inside to use the restroom. She never came out, so I went in to see if she was alright. I locked the car before going in. I couldn't find her and came back outside, and my car was gone."

"Sounds like you missed her and she took the car," the officer said. "You two on good terms?"

"Yes, great terms. We have only been married about a year. Our relationship couldn't be better."

"Right," the officer said, doubt in his voice, or was it concern? "Let's take you to the station where you can file an official report. It is about a fifteen-minute drive into town. Are you sure your wife won't return with the car and start to worry about you?"

"She is not going to come back with the car," Jack said, exasperated.

"So you two had a fight?" the officer asked. "Where would she have taken the vehicle?"

"She did not take the car, officer," Jack said. "I have the only key," he added pulling the keys from his right pants pocket.

"So you keep the keys from her?" the officer asked. "You don't trust her? Had she threatened to leave recently?"

"No officer," Jack said, exasperated.

"So you don't trust her. Why is that?" the officer asked as he opened the passenger door for Jack.

Jack just rolled his eyes as he got in the patrol car. They didn't talk as they drove to the station. Jack looked in every direction as they entered the town.

CHAPTER 2
MINA

MONDAY
14 SEPTEMBER 2015, 6:37 A.M.

"I WILL BE RIGHT BACK," MINA said. "I just want to get a bottle of water and some gum to help me stay awake. You want anything?"

"Yeah, get me a bottle of water too, and a bag of Cheetos," Jack said. Mina could feel Jack's eyes on her as she walked into the gas station convenience store. She smiled as she opened the front door. She picked a few snacks and two bottles of water. She almost forgot the Cheetos and grabbed them on her way to the cashier counter. She adored Jack's childlike love of Cheetos. Not that the snack was anything special, but it had brought them together. Mina remembered the first time they met. They had reached for the same bag of Cheetos at a grocery store in Palo Alto, California. A health conscious city, they were both surprised they were actually in competition for this sack of twenty grams of fat and 700 milligrams of sodium. Jack had said, "Well now you know my worst vice, you should feel safe sharing this bag with me." Mina had smiled and uncharacteristically agreed to this serendipitous date with this tall, handsome Viking. He wasn't as muscle-bound as the Thor in the superhero movies, but she thought his blonde hair and light brown eyes made him much more attractive than some comic book warrior. She would find out on their first date that he had a slight English accent and was from Yorkshire, England of an English father and American mother. She would find out when she met his parents that his father did come from Vikings that arrived on Britain with the Norman Conquest. The next fifteen months of dating and marriage had been a blissful experience, even with the challenges of married finances, the new job offer, and the move.

Mina walked to the bathroom and then decided to take the bag to the car before using the bathroom that would disgust a 13th-century peasant. Jack was apparently daydreaming. The pump had stopped, and Jack was just standing there.

"Mina to Jack, the tank is full," Mina said pulling him out of his thoughts. "All systems go for permission to reenter earth's atmosphere."

Jack pulled the nozzle out of the gas tank opening and inserted it back in its holder. He replaced the tank cap before speaking. "Thanks, Mina," Jack began. "I was just thinking about our firsts. I suppose I am just getting tired, but my mind didn't want to shift back to the present. You got my Cheetos, right?

"Yes, I got your precious Cheetos," Mina said smiling. "Firsts, huh. I thought you said you were getting tired." Mina leaned against the car in an attempt at a sexy pose. She knew that wasn't her forte and that she probably only looked silly. She loved this Cheetos obsessed man and didn't mind looking silly.

Jack grabbed Mina and held her tight. He gave her a long kiss while secretly trying to reach for the bag of snacks Mina held in her left hand. Jack's strong body felt good, and she smiled as Jack brushed away her hair from her face. She looked into his light blue eyes and could see the ocean they had left behind for their move to Minneapolis. Jack shook her out of her own day-dream saying, "You know I probably fell in love with you because you have these tiny orange flecks in your eyes that look just like Cheetos."

Mina punched him in the stomach playfully and pulled the snack bag away from his clutches. She ran around to the passenger door of the 1987 Saab 900. "I am going back in to use the restroom, which I should have visited before buying the food. It's filthy, and there was nowhere to set the bag. If you are good and don't eat all the snacks before I get back, I will give you a special prize." She tossed the bag through the passenger window and returned to the store.

Mina knew he was going to eat the Cheetos and still plead for a special prize. She also knew she would relent and offer him a choice of a second bag she had put in her purse, or herself in the teddy she had purchased as a house warming present to Jack once they got to their destination. One more night in a motel, probably in Omaha, that is if they could get through the rest of Wyoming and Nebraska today. Maybe they would celebrate their last night on the road instead.

She was surprised when Jack ran up to her and said, "I decided I'd better use the restroom too."

"You go first then," Mina said. "I might take a few minutes. I will check out the fishing guides I noticed, for my cousin."

Jack shrugged his shoulders and went into the bathroom.

Mina smiled as he walked toward the restroom, hoping he was prepared mentally for the cesspool failing to masquerade as a human bathroom. She didn't see him leave the bathroom, but she had been engrossed in the fishing guides. Knocking on the restroom door, no one answered, so she took a breath and entered, figuring Jack had returned to the car. She completed her business and was glad to leave the store and get as far away from that restroom as possible. As she exited, she was surprised to not see the car by the pump. She looked right and left to where Jack had parked. She didn't see the car anywhere. She walked around the back of the store and saw nothing but a dumpster and some barrels by the back door.

"Okay Jack, very funny," Mina said out loud while she tried to make sense of this. She searched through her purse for her cell phone, feeling her anxiety rise. She knew this was a joke, but she didn't find it at all funny. She clicked on Jack's number from her favorites list. It rang and rang with no reply. She marched back to the front door and looked inside, just in case. Jack was nowhere to be found. Mina sat down on the curb and waited, not sure what to do next. Twenty minutes into her wait she walked out to the road and looked in both directions, hoping to see their car broke down just within site. Nothing. She waited another twenty minutes and then talked to the cashier in the convenience store. He had a three or four-day growth of a beard, and he had on a baseball cap that shadowed much of his face. She was a little afraid to disturb him.

"What would be the closest town to here?" Mina asked.

"That would be Arlington," the man said looking up at her, his eyes seeming to look right through her to the far wall.

"Do they have a police station?" Mina asked.

"Mam, I think there are about twenty-five people in the town, and they are all law abiding citizens. The nearest police would be in Laramie. They have local police, county sheriffs, and a Highway Patrol Port of Entry weigh station,"

"Thank you," Mina said as she turned to go. She didn't like the feeling of the cashier looking at her as she left. She walked away from the door where she was out of the view of the guy and considered her options. There was an older lady getting gas, but otherwise, the place was empty. She could call 911, but what would she tell the police? "My husband abandoned me or got kidnapped? What would happen when Jack shows up, and the police have come to investigate? Would they arrest him for his ill-planned joke?"

Mina walked over to the lady just finishing her fill-up and asked, "Excuse me, mam, could I ask you a question?"

The woman looked at Mina and must have decided she looked safe to talk to. "What can I do for you?" she asked.

"My husband and I stopped here for gas about an hour ago, maybe less, and when I came out of the restroom, he was gone."

"I don't know which is worse," the lady said. "Using that restroom or discovering your husband has abandoned you."

"Oh, he didn't abandon me, I am sure," Mina said. "He is probably playing a really dumb joke, and he is in big trouble for that. I was wondering, what direction are you going?"

"I am heading back to my ranch," the lady said.

"Is there any chance I could get a ride to Laramie if your ranch is that direction," Mina said. "I know that is a crazy request. I can pay for the gas. I just don't want to stay here by myself waiting for my husband or for the police if I decide to call them. That cashier makes me nervous." Mina looked closely at this older lady for the first time. Her face had wrinkles and was witness to a lot of sun and wind. Her hair was graying and cut simple at the shoulder. She had very kind eyes, and Mina felt strength in them.

The lady at the pump studied Mina another minute and finally said, "Hop in. There are days when I think I would be doing the world a favor by shooting Jacob. He is probably harmless, but to offer that bathroom and "don't talk to me" attitude to unsuspecting travelers who will remember that above any other Wyoming memory is a federal crime."

"Thank you. My name is Mina, Mina Gamble."

"My name is McKenzie," the lady said. "I have to go by my place first, but that won't take much time, then I can run you into Laramie. I got a spread just east of the Little Laramie River. They say Wyoming is the least populated state in the country, but I get the heebeegeebees going into a big city like Laramie, so I put up with Jacob for gas and the few necessities I can get here.

Mina wasn't sure this was the best idea, to leave here. She was certain she didn't want to stay here alone with Jacob, so she hopped in the jeep with McKenzie and buckled her seat belt.

CHAPTER 3
JACOB

MONDAY
14 SEPTEMBER 2015, 6:37 A.M.

JACOB WAS DAYDREAMING OF THE fishing trip he had planned for the upcoming weekend. He and his dog Beau, a Bouvier he had trained as a herding dog for the sheep he ran on the twelve acres he rented, were planning on checking out Grays Reef of the North Platte. His thoughts were interrupted by the door chime. He already knew it was one of the fifty or sixty customers his gas station serviced every day. Jacob was always surprised how many people forgot to get gas in one of the more major towns along Interstate 80. Situated between Rawlins and Laramie, Jacob made a fair living as that emergency gas stop. He used to also run a tow truck service but got tired of having an extra employee around, even though the service paid for itself and then some.

This customer was memorable. She was young and beautiful. Her curly dark hair reminded him of Beau. Her athletic body and how she walked certainly did not remind him of his dog, however. She bought a few snack items and paid for them hardly without looking at him. Few people had ever looked at him. She then walked to the restroom, but was only there for a few seconds. Jacob braced himself for the typical complaints, but she walked past him out to her car. He watched her walk past the view of his outdoor security camera and assumed she had decided to drive on to the next town.

He had just put a plastic spoon in a freshly opened a can of pork and beans that would be his lunch when the young lady returned. She had obviously changed her mind. A man talked with her and he went to the restroom. She walked over to the fishing guides. Jacob went back to his beans and American Angler Magazine he was devouring.

* * *

Just as Jacob finished his can of beans and most of the magazine articles a young man walked into the store obviously upset. He walked to the restrooms and Jacob watched him knock on the women's room. No answer. "Mina, it's Jack. You okay?" the guy said. He tried the door, and it was unlocked. He knocked again and called out the name Mina again. Jacob was beginning to really enjoy this, wondering if this person was connected to that cute lady that had been here. 'How long ago was that?' he wondered. The man slowly opened the door again. "Mina?" he said once again, to an empty bathroom. Jacob was reminded of the definition of crazy his daddy used to pronounce to his children. "Crazy is when you do the same thing again and expect a different result."

Jacob watched more carefully as Jack hurriedly looked around the store. The middle aged woman looking at selections in the candy aisle and a man, probably her husband, grabbing some water bottles were a little concerned about this guy, and they quickly made their purchases and left. Jack turned to Jacob and asked, "Did you see a young lady, twenty-five years old, shoulder length brunette hair walk in here a few minutes ago?"

Jacob looked at the clock on the wall, just over the alcove where the bathrooms were. The time really didn't help him. Jacob could lose hours when he was reading. And he was always reading. "I haven't seen any young women in over an hour," Jacob said, trying to remember again when that cute young lady had been in the store. "Believe me, I would have noticed. This is the most boring part of the day."

"Is there another exit, a back door?" Jack asked starting to panic and making Jacob nervous.

"There is a delivery entrance, but we don't use it. That door has been padlocked for years. It's hard enough to secure the front doors," Jacob explained.

Mind if I check it?" Jack asked.

Jacob was about to say no but saw the anxiety in Jack's face. "Go ahead, but if you take more than fifteen seconds, I am coming back looking for you."

Jacob hadn't told him there was a security camera that covered the back door. He watched Jack run to the back door and found that it was locked just as Jacob said. Jacob was about to walk to the back as Jack started poking around the back room. Jack walked back out to the front of the store and walked down the three junk food aisles confirming in Jacob's mind that this guy was a few gallons short of a full tank. Jack walked outside.

""What the..?" Jack said loud enough for Jacob to hear it before the door closed. "Is this some kind of joke? Where is the camera?" Jacob watched Jack look around and then stare directly at the camera and then walk back inside.

"Could I view your outside security camera? Either my wife has taken the car as a joke, or it has been stolen," Jack asked.

"My camera only goes a few feet out the door, but you are welcome to look at it," Jacob said. "It only holds a digital recording of about two hours in length and then starts recording over itself."

"That is enough time," Jack said. Jack and Jacob watched a lady come in the store and then nearly forty-five minutes later they saw Jack come in the store and then go out. Jack appeared mixed up. Jacob that maybe he was on drugs. Jack walked around the back of the gas station and back to the front. He walked back inside and didn't even ask permission to go to the back of the store one more time. Jack rechecked both bathrooms and behind the counter. "I need to make a phone call," he said to Jacob. "My car was just stolen, and my wife is missing. My cell phone was in the car."

"Are you sure your wife didn't take the car?" Jacob said while trying to stifle a laugh. This was the most entertaining day he had experienced in at least a month. "You wouldn't be the first to get dumped at this gas station. Well, maybe you are the first," Jacob said.

Jack continued to look at Jacob. He was a big man. Unkempt, with rough cut dark hair and a gnarly beard. His clothes looked clean but looked like they had been wadded up for a year before this guy put them on this morning. He had some of the biggest hands Jack had ever seen. "Okay, you can make a 911 call. I don't want to be stuck with you all day," Jacob said.

The police arrived twenty minutes later. They found Jack sitting on the curb in the parking lot. Jacob watched them talk to Jack and then Jack got in their car and left.

* * *

No sooner had the police car disappeared down the road, then the young lady, 'Mina was what the guy had been calling here, right?' Jacob thought, came out of the bathroom and walked outside.

As she exited, she was surprised to not see the car by the pump. She looked right and left to where Jack had parked. She didn't see the car anywhere. She walked around the back of the store and saw nothing but a dumpster and some barrels by the back door.

"Okay Jack, hilarious," Mina said loud enough for Jacob to hear, even with the glass front door now closed. He watched her grab her cell phone and make a call. Apparently, it either wasn't working. Or no one answered. Mina peeked inside and then sat down on the curb outside the store. Jacob and the lady waited for something to happen for about twenty minutes. Jacob had decided against getting involved. That was pretty much his motto and why he lived alone in the middle of the least populous state in the country. After another few minutes, Mina came into the store to talk with Jacob.

"What would be the closest town to here?" Mina asked.

"That would be Arlington," Jacob said, trying not to think through what elaborate game this girl and her guy friend were playing.

"Do they have a police station?" Mina asked.

"Mam, I think there are about twenty-five people in the town, and they are all law abiding citizens. The nearest police would be in Laramie. They have local police, county sheriffs, and a Highway Patrol Port of Entry weigh station," Jacob explained.

"Thank you," Mina said as she turned to go. Jacob watched her go out to talk with McKenzie, one of the local ranchers who was at the gas pumps.

Mina and McKenzie talked for a few minutes and Jacob was surprised to see Mina get in the car with McKenzie and they drove off. Jacob waited for Jack or Mina to show up again, but no one ever did. Jacob closed up the store and left the pumps on auto as he contemplated the fishing that would challenge, entertain, and feed him and Beau over the next couple of days.

CHAPTER 4
MCKENZIE

MONDAY
14 SEPTEMBER 2015, 8:13 A.M.

" **I** 'M DOWN TO JUST BELOW a half tank in the Jeep," McKenzie told her twelve goats that were baying for her attention. "I will feed you when I get back. Shouldn't be more than an hour. You'll live."

McKenzie never liked to be lower than half a tank in her primary vehicle, but today she had another reason to leave her ranch and visit Jacob's gas station. She had a Honda four-track, an Arctic snowmobile, and an ancient Piper Cub aircraft that hadn't left the ground in over twenty years, but the Jeep was her go-to transportation. Living forty miles from the closest gas station and nearly double that to the nearest big town that offered medical care and other emergency necessities, she tried to always be prepared. Some of her neighbors had gas tanks on their ranch, but McKenzie didn't see the need for her small ranch operation. And with the closest neighbor being about twenty miles away, she didn't want to depend on them in an emergency either. In the summer, like today, she was a little more lax about the level of her tank, but in the winter she carried four extra five-gallon canisters with her, that supplemented her extra-large factory installed gas tank.

Not one to leave things to chance, McKenzie had a year's supply of food, animal feed for three months, and a 2,500-gallon water tank supplied by her well. She wasn't a survivalist, but she wasn't one of those city folks who thought food would always just magically appear in the grocery stores. McKenzie enjoyed the trip to and from the gas station, even though she didn't much care for the guy that owned it, Jacob Critchlow. Her drive would take her through and past her 500-acre spread and she could do a little people watching at the gas station. There were weeks when those were the only people she saw. Besides her ranch animals, consisting of her goats, fourteen laying chickens, and her buffalo herd, the occasional prong-horned antelope and a sage grouse were the only other creatures with whom she crossed paths.

She arrived at the gas station just as a car with a couple in it drove off and without much else to see. No other cars were there, but there was this nervous looking young lady that had come in and out of the store a couple of times. Surely she wasn't Jacob's girlfriend. Was she stranded, or waiting for a ride from someone? How in the world did she end up at this bump in the road? Although McKenzie liked the solitary life-style of a Wyoming rancher, she was aware most did not. That was all right with her. She didn't want what cities offered, but she recognized, even from a distance, this young lady did. McKenzie slowed her gas purchase to see what was going on.

When the young lady approached McKenzie, her caution heightened. "Excuse me, mam, could I ask you a question?" the young lady asked.

McKenzie looked at the young lady trying to decide if this was some sort of scam operation. "What can I do for you?" McKenzie asked.

"My husband and I stopped here for gas about an hour ago, maybe less, and when I came out of the restroom, he was gone."

"I don't know which is worse," McKenzie said. "Using that restroom, or discovering your husband has abandoned you." McKenzie wanted to laugh at her little joke, but it was obvious this lady was about to fall apart.

"Oh, he didn't abandon me, I am sure," the young lady said. "He is probably playing a really dumb joke, and he is in big trouble for that. I was wondering, what direction are you going?"

"I am heading back to my ranch," McKenzie said.

"Is there any chance I could get a ride to Laramie if you are going that direction?" the young lady asked. "I know that is a crazy request. I can pay for the gas. I just don't want to stay here by myself waiting for my husband, or for the police if I decide to call them. That cashier makes me nervous."

McKenzie studied the young lady another minute. She seemed bright and was obviously pretty. McKenzie carried a weapon with her, mostly for rattlesnakes and the like, but this girl didn't. Jacob was not a danger to society, except if you took into account his total lack of hygiene, but she didn't want to leave this girl out here by herself. Finally, McKenzie said, "Hop in. There are days when I think I would be doing the world a favor by shooting Jacob. He is probably harmless, but to offer that bathroom to unsuspecting travelers who will remember that above any other Wyoming memory is a federal crime."

"Thank you. My name is Mina, Mina Gamble," the young lady said.

"My name's McKenzie. I have to go by my place first, but that won't take much time, then I can run you into Laramie. I got a spread just east of Cooper Mountain. They say Wyoming is the least populated state in the country, but I get the heebeegeebees going into a big city like Laramie, so I put up with Jacob for gas and the few necessities I can get here."

McKenzie could see Mina weighing her options and soon hopped in the Jeep with McKenzie and buckled her seat belt.

McKenzie tried to start up a conversation a couple of times, but she had never been very good at that. "I'm sorry," Mina said. "I am not trying to be rude, but I can't get my head around what has happened in the last hour. My husband has disappeared, and I am abandoned in the middle of Wyoming. No offense, to Wyoming, but this place is pretty desolate."

"Wyoming is less frequented, and it is a little isolated if that is your definition of desolate, but I like to think of it as thick in the thinness between heaven and earth, and thin in the thick-headedness that populates most cities," McKenzie said. When that seemed to shut down Mina's attempt at conversation, McKenzie said, "I'm sorry. Don't listen to this old rancher. I don't get a lot of practice with my conversation skills. By the way, we just entered my property. See those brown dots on that mesa?" McKenzie asked.

"Yes, Mina said, only half-heartedly in the conversation.

"Those are my Buffalo. Fifty head, with about half destined for supermarkets and restaurants in the intermountain west before summer hits its peak."

"Oh wow," Mina said. "I have never eaten buffalo. I don't think I have ever even seen it in the store."

"It is a growing trend, and let me tell you, it is tasty and better for you. I know you are in a hurry to find your husband but are you hungry? All this talk of food has started to tickle my tummy. How about it?"

"Thank you, but I couldn't impose," Mina said. "Besides, I need to get to Laramie."

When was the last time you ate?" McKenzie asked.

I had some Cheetos at the gas station," Mina said starting to cry. "They were a surprise for Jack, my husband. I was starving."

"Well I wouldn't count Cheetos as real food Missy," McKenzie said. "It will only take a few minutes to rustle us up some grub, and I can get you to Laramie right after that. You want to take care of yourself, so you can be on top of things. It may be a long night too." Mina looked exhausted, and McKenzie hoped a little food in her stomach was just what she needed.

They pulled up to a white two-story ranch house. The hitching posts just off the front porch made the scene look like it was on the set of Bonanza. "Let me get you something to drink while I get the food," McKenzie said.

Mina walked up the steps to the raised wooden porch that looked like it completely surrounded the house. There was a small barn and what looked like another shed. A few large oak trees provided some shade, but otherwise, it was clear of large growth for miles. Inside the house was tidy and used. The furniture was not new but looked clean and sturdy. There was a family picture on the mantle above the fireplace in the main room, and the large windows provided plenty of light. Mina felt comforted that she hadn't stepped into the Cabin in the Woods. She hadn't seen the movie but guessed it was the rural version of the Bates Motel. McKenzie's place, on the other hand, brought the first peace to Mina's heart since she discovered their car gone and presumably her husband with it. Mina sat down on the love seat that faced the big window facing some mountains and started again sorting through the events of the past few hours.

"Here's some food Mina," McKenzie said. "I am going to feed the goats, so we can get to Laramie and find your husband."

Mina walked to the table and saw two plates of food. Steak, cheese, and tomatoes. Mina was halfway through her steak when McKenzie returned. "This is delicious McKenzie," Mina said. "I am embarrassed I am so hungry."

"Wyoming air will do that to you," McKenzie said as she finished washing her hands. "That is a buffalo steak from my herd, and the cheese is homemade from my goats. The tomatoes I grew and picked this morning. Jehoshaphat!" McKenzie exclaimed. "I love eating food I grow myself. The Czar of Russia doesn't eat this good." McKenzie was through with her plate about the same time as Mina. They hopped in the Jeep and once again were racing across the Wyoming steppes, this time headed for Laramie.

CHAPTER 5
JACK

MONDAY
14 SEPTEMBER 2015, 10:03 A.M.

"YOU SAY YOUR NAME IS Jack Gamble. Do you have any identification?" The police officer at the desk asked. "It's not that we don't trust you, but it is standard procedure. You wouldn't believe what nuts travel through the Cowboy State."

Jack was looking at several license plates tacked on the wall. The slogan stated, "Like No Place On Earth." He could certainly agree with that. Feeling a little nauseous, Jack looked around for a place to sit down. The reality of the situation was hitting him hard. Mina had just disappeared. Every possible danger he had ever read or seen in the movies was passing through his mind. "Officer," Jack look at his name tag, "Officer Cochran, would it be alright with you if I sat down for a minute?"

"That would be fine Mr. Gamble," the officer said as he handed Jack back his driver's license. "We will need to do a routine blood test, but only if you agree to it," the officer added.

"This is not about me, officer," Jack said, getting mad. "What does it matter what is or isn't in my blood? My wife is missing. She may be hurt, or kidnapped." He couldn't bring himself to verbalize all his thoughts.

"Like I said, there are some real nut cases that stand just where you are standing. Before we dedicate our resources, we have a few procedural steps to cover. No problem about the sobriety test, though."

"Well, go ahead," Jack said. "Let's get this over with. I don't want any doubts about what I am saying or my mental health, or whatever. I want you to find my wife."

"I'm afraid the blood test doesn't cover mental health," Officer Cochran said with a chuckle. "I sure wish it did. That would make a lot of these cases much simpler. It will just take a second." He picked up the phone and asked another officer to take him into another room for the blood test. The room smelled of ink and beer. With a second breath, he realized it was the remains of someone's throw-up. That put him over the edge, and he grabbed the trash can under the fingerprint table and emptied his stomach. When he lifted his head to apologize, he saw the officer he had been talking to and another officer staring at him, both trying to hide a disgusted look. He apologized anyway.

"Don't worry about it, Mr. Gamble. This room sees a lot of that," Officer Cochran said. The other officer finished swabbing Jack's arm and stuck a needle in a vein in his arm like an experienced nurse in the ER, minus any bedside manner. The needle came out, and a bandage slapped on about the same time Jack's head started to return to normal.

"We'll have the results in half an hour," the second officer said. "If you can wait until then before leaving, that would help us if we need to find you."

"Wait, Jack said, "I am not going anywhere because I don't have a car and I can't find my wife. I don't think my bloodwork is going to help in either case, so can we get to the point of why I called you and why I am here."

"We can take you to the Motel 6 about a block away, and you can wait there," Officer Cochran said. "If we hear from your wife, we will know where to find you. Chances are, she will call here looking for you. We'll let the County Sherriff's Office and the Highway Patrol know the details as well, in case she contacts them. Usually, you would have been picked up by a deputy, but they were busy, and we weren't so we were happy to help out."

"Thank you, officer," Jack said. I need to get to town and buy a phone and call parents and friends in case she has contacted them."

"I can drop you off at the T-Mobile store just up 3rd. Too far to walk," Cochran said. "You'll have to find your way to a motel from there on your own. Once you get a number, give us a call, and we can add it to your information and be able to contact you easier."

Jack ended up at a Verizon store just across the street from where Officer Cochran dropped him off since he already had an account with them. He reported his phone stolen and got a new one with the same number. That kept things simple, so he didn't have to give his family, friends and work a new number. The first thing he did was try to call Mina. No answer and Verizon confirmed they hadn't registered any usage on her number over the past two days. They also confirmed it must be off or the battery was dead as they didn't find it in their system. No one in the family had heard from Mina either, and only her mother expressed any concern. Everyone assured him she was either playing a joke or somehow missed him when he went into the gas station store. This was just too weird to be anything else. He also contacted his new job in Minneapolis and told them his car was stolen. They told him to take a couple more days, and they would see him in the office on Thursday, four days from now.

While Jack sat eating a wood fired pizza at the Alibi Pub, he sorted out his options. He just couldn't get past the fact that Mina was here, somewhere. He could feel it. He had no intentions of leaving until he found her. He tried to control his thoughts and worries about her, but he failed about every two or three minutes. "Could she have been abducted? Did she have her purse with her? Yes, that was in the car, right? Or did she take into the restroom with her? I can't remember. If she were robbed, why would they take her too? A sicko? Like the cop said, lots of strange people passing through Wyoming. Man, I hope none of them stopped here today." He continued to talk to himself until his phone rang.

"Hello," he answered, praying to hear Mina's voice on the other end of the line. "Jack, this is mom."

"Hey mom, you hear from Mina?" Jack asked.

"Well, no honey," his mom began. "It seems the police in Laramie tracked you to us. They said they found your car, abandoned at a gas station. They had to break into it and the car registration still has our address on it. Mina was not there. You need to contact the police. You haven't given them your number?"

"No mom," Jack said. "My phone was in the car when it got stolen. I guess whoever took it kept the phone, but didn't want to get caught with the car. I bought a new phone. I will give the police a call. I feel like I am in the Twilight Zone. One step closer to finding Mina and getting out of this place. Thanks, I will after I get some of this sorted out."

Jack called the police, and they sent a squad car to pick him up. Fifteen minutes later he was back at the station.

"Good news Mr. Gamble," Officer Cochran said when he stepped back into the building. Jack's heart soared. "Your blood test came back negative, you're clean."

"I knew that," James said. "That is hardly good news considering my wife is still missing. So my mom called and told me you found my car at a gas station. What shape is it in?"

"Your car?" Cochran asked. "You found it?"

"No, you did," Jack corrected.

"Hmm, maybe the Sherriff's Office or the Highway Patrol," Cochran said. "I will give them a call." He speed-dialed one and talked for a briefly to someone, then called the other number. Less than a minute later he hung up the phone and asked, "Who told you we found your car?"

"My mother, in California," Jack said. "She told me she got a call from this office."

"Did she give you a name?" Cochran asked. "Sounds like some bored punks playing with you."

Jack called his mom and told her what was going on. She repeated exactly what was said in the phone call and even named Officer Cochran. Jack handed the phone to Cochran, and she repeated her call once again. Officer Cochran gave the phone back to Jack and said, "Either this is some elaborate joke, or you are hiding something. It isn't funny taking up our time with this. I suggest you start with the truth Mr. Gamble. We know nothing about your car, or if you even have a wife, or for that matter, if you really even have a car, or if that was really your mother I was talking to."

Jack was speechless. His mom never lied and how could she have come up with some story about his car, and the name of this investigator? You're correct officer, something is not right here. I can't explain it, but this morning my wife and I stopped to get gas, now my car is gone, my wife is gone, my mother, who isn't playing a joke, called and told me you called her. She had your number and your name. Maybe it is you who is playing the joke here."

"Be careful where you go with accusations against a police officer Mr. Gamble," Cochran said. "We don't joke around, at least not on duty. Like I said, some punk could have easily passed on my name and number. I can think of plenty who have darkened our doorway and would love to create an issue against us, or me in particular. Hopefully, the caller will tire of this game and your car and wife will show up. If you or anyone in your family gets another call, get as much information as you can. If this game goes on much longer, I will issue a missing person's report, and after that, we'll get the FBI involved. I assume you are going to stay in Laramie tonight then?"

"Yes, I am staying here," Jack said. "You've got my number, so you can reach me anytime, as soon as you hear anything. Sorry for the accusation. I am really frazzled."

"Understandable," Cochran said.

CHAPTER 6
MINA

MINA AND MCKENZIE STOPPED FIRST at the Sherriff's Office. The deputies obviously knew McKenzie well and treated her with obvious respect, almost as if their mom was visiting. They had heard nothing about a missing car, nor had Jack contacted them. Their next stop was the Highway Patrol. Nothing. Their last stop was the Laramie City Police. Officer Cochran was at the desk. Mina instinctively didn't like this man. He was lean but looked strong. His head was shaved, and he had a farmer's tan on his forehead where his hat must cover his head. He had a bored, but on edge look, like he was too important to be worried, but something was eating at him.

"McKenzie," Officer Cochran said as both ladies walked in the door. "What brings you to the big city?"

"My friend here, Mina Gamble is worried about her husband," McKenzie said. "I was out at Jacob's getting gas and found her stranded there. Her husband and their car disappeared. Honey, you tell your story."

Mina explained what had happened while Officer Cochran took notes.

"So there is no reason your husband would've just up and left you?" Cochran asked. "Not in a fight, or some other reason. Please be honest, so we can help you get to the bottom of this."

"No reason," Mina said. "Things between us are great. Could he have been kidnapped, or carjacked? I mean both him and the car gone." She couldn't get any more words out. She was starting to fall apart, and she didn't want to do that in front of these strangers. She had thought that if she could just get to the police, they would have the answers and this would all be sorted out. That was obviously not happening. Maybe because this was her last stop, but she wasn't sure, but what she was feeling in her heart was, she didn't like Officer Cochran.

"I tell you what," Officer Cochran said, "you stay with McKenzie for the time being, and when your husband comes looking for you, which I am sure he will do, I will know who to contact."

"That's it?" Mina asked. No report to fill out? No other suggestions? This is our last stop." She began to cry.

"Mam," Cochran said. "I am sorry, but we have to wait forty-eight hours in this kind of situation before we can begin a missing persons process, that is unless you saw your husband abducted."

"No," Mina said. "I didn't see him get abducted."

"Come on Missy," McKenzie said, putting her arm around Mina for support and guiding her toward the door. "Let me take you home and maybe we'll get a call by the time we get there."

McKenzie and Mina stayed in their own worlds of thought on the drive. They were back at McKenzie's place forty-five minutes later. One thing Mina was certain of, Jack was still here, somewhere.

"Okay honey, we need to put you to work," McKenzie said as she got out of her truck. "You go collect the eggs out of the hen house. There is a basket by the pen door. I usually have that done by now, but well, it's not been a regular day has it?"

Mina walked toward the chicken pen. She grabbed the basket, opened the pen gate, closed it and stooped as she entered the hen house. Something like twelve hens were nestled, ready for the cool summer night. The coop was clean and warm. Each displayed varying degrees of indignation to her intrusion. A few broody hens were very protective, and she had to use the rounded wooden handle of a nearby pitchfork to push them off their nests to check for eggs. She wasn't sure that was the right thing to do, but it was safer than getting pecked to death and gave her focus. Eighteen eggs, some brown, some white. "What does McKenzie do with all these eggs?" Mina asked the birds. It was obviously a secret the hens were not going to divulge. They tried to pretend she wasn't there. "Maybe that's it," Mina told the hens. "So I'm not really here. What if Jack is actually looking for me and can't find me?" If any of the hens know the answer to that, they weren't sharing.

As Mina exited the chicken coop, McKenzie was standing by the pen door with her hands on her hips, staring at Mina. It spooked her, and she almost dropped the basket. "I sell most of 'em," McKenzie said. "It's okay; I talk to the hens too. Sometimes they offer some pretty good answers if the questions are about the weather. Chickens have a brain the size of a pea, but I think they think about the future, maybe even worry about it."

"They certainly worry about protecting their eggs," Mina offered as she handed the basket to McKenzie.

"That might not be a thought, just something wired in," McKenzie said. "Otherwise, why keep laying eggs if they knew they would be taken. Let's put these in the frig in the barn. It keeps the eggs fresh until I can get 'em to town, about every two weeks. The frig is also a good insulator—keeps 'em from freezing in the winter."

Mina followed McKenzie to the barn. After the eggs were transferred to cartons and put in cold storage, McKenzie turned to Mina and asked, "So what was that other conversation you were having?"

"I don't know," Mina answered, not sure what McKenzie was asking.

"About you not really being here," McKenzie said.

"Oh, just a random thought," Mina said trying to smile to assure McKenzie she wasn't a nut case.

"Interesting idea actually," McKenzie said sitting on a ball of straw. "Tell me about it."

"Just a thought, really nothing," Mina said, trying to think of something else to change the subject. "Is that an old car?" Mina asked, pointing at a car shape under a canvas tarp at the far end of the barn.

"My husband's," McKenzie said. "It may be crazy, or seem silly, but I want to hear about your thought."

Mina took a deep breath and almost choked on the musty air of the barn. "I can't explain what happened today. Jack wouldn't leave me. I'm not saying that out of naiveté or stupidity. Outside of being carjacked, I don't have a logical explanation."

"But you do have another explanation?" McKenzie asked.

"Kind of," Mina said. "It's not an explanation really, just a feeling."

"Try it out on me," McKenzie said with a cautious smile. "I'm a pretty good listener."

"I'm not sure I can put it into words really," Mina said. "I know Jack. He wouldn't leave me. So if he didn't leave me what are the options? One is, he was taken against his will."

"That is a possibility," McKenzie said. "We can get back to the possibility that your husband is a flake and you never knew it, and he just took off. The car was gone too, right?"

"Yes!" Mina yelled. "The car is gone too. I know that seems like the obvious answer to Jack's disappearance, but it's NOT. He did not leave me. Short of being car-jacked, he did not leave that gas station."

"I don't see any other answer sweetie," McKenzie said wanting to hug this poor, very much alone young lady.

"Humor me," Mina said. "There are other answers. What about Jack being robbed and taken along with his car?"

"Honey," McKenzie said, "this is Wyoming. It's not Chicago, New York, or Los Angeles. There's about as good a chance that he was abducted by aliens."

"Exactly," Mina said, not sounding quite that sure. "What if, what if Jack is looking for me and I am looking for him?"

"That could be, but you would almost have to be looking in different places, and our little patch of sky just isn't that big," McKenzie said, not sounding quite so sure herself either Mina thought.

"It's like we are in separate worlds," Mina almost whispered. "I will not stop looking for him, but I have this feeling that I could look forever and never find him." Mina began to sob quietly, trying to hold in all her ache, frustration, and fear of being alone.

"Well, you've come to the right place then," McKenzie said, sitting down by Mina to give her a comforting hug. "Why don't you take a little nap and we can talk when you are fresh."

"I don't want to sleep," Mina said through choppy breaths. "I don't think I will be able to ever sleep again, actually." She cried softly for another minute, and within two minutes she was asleep in McKenzie's arms. McKenzie gently laid her down on the couch where they were both sitting. She put a fleece blanket over Mina and quietly left the room, trying to gather her own thoughts.

Mina woke up to silence. Not just quiet, but peaceful silence. She knew exactly where she was and that she was alone, in the middle of Wyoming. Before she started to cry again, she pulled herself off the couch and stood up, taking in all the air her lungs could hold. As she slowly let out her breath, she looked around McKenzie's living room for the first time. She was specifically drawn to a photo of a man and a women sitting on the mantle of the fireplace. The warmth of the fire felt good. The young lady in the picture could be McKenzie long ago, or perhaps her daughter. A yellowed piece of paper, apparently torn from a larger piece of paper, held the hand-written words, *There is one who scatters, and yet increases all the more, And there is one who withholds what is justly due, and yet it results only in want. Psalms 11:24.* Under the quote were the letters *FWLK.*

"That's me and Frank," McKenzie said, startling Mina.

"Oh, I'm sorry," Mina said. "I didn't mean to be nosey. The fire felt warm and then I saw the picture." She dismissed the initials as those of McKenzie's husband.

"No worries Missy," McKenzie said smiling. "If I didn't want people seeing it, I would've put it somewhere more private. We had just moved onto the ranch, about 22 years ago. Sold everything and moved to the wide open spaces."

"I can see the excitement in your eyes, both of you," Mina said, wanting to ask about McKenzie's husband, but didn't. She settled on the simple statement, "And now you run this place alone."

"Oh, Frank is still here, at least I like to think so," McKenzie said now forcing a smile.

Mina wasn't sure how to respond to that, so she turned to look at the other walls in the cozy living room. No other photographs. A quilt hung on one wall, and a few paintings adorned the others.

"You won't find any answers on these walls," McKenzie said. "This is my public space. Not that I entertain much of the public.

Come on upstairs, and I will show you what I think you are looking for."

"Oh, I'm not looking for anything," Mina said, surprised. "I guess I am just trying to get acquainted and give my mind time to think about what my next step should be to find Jack."

"Exactly," McKenzie said. "Come on up the stairs, Missy. You might be from the big city, and I live a pretty solitary life here, but we have a lot more in common than you think."

Mina followed McKenzie up the stairs. The only voice was the creaking stairs that complained of having two people ascending them instead of the typical one. McKenzie passed the first door and opened a door on the left side of the simple hallway. That door creaked in complaint as well. It felt to Mina like the whole house was unhappy with her presence. Mina followed McKenzie inside the room. She was immediately on guard.

"This was operations central back in the day," McKenzie said with a sweep of her hand. "Now I just come her now and then to think and dream of what might have been."

The walls of the room were filled with pictures and notes tacked on top of each other. The entire wall opposite the two windows that looked out onto the farmyard was covered with a chalkboard. It was filled with formulas and a few diagrams that made no sense to Mina. There was only one chair and two long tables stacked with papers, books, and more photos. Mina feared she had walked into a schizophrenic's mind. The only thing that strangely seemed normal was a massive telescope pointed to the ceiling. As Mina looked at the ceiling she noticed the ceiling could be retracted and the telescope could pivot in almost any direction.

"Sorry for the shock," McKenzie said, studying Mina. "I know it looks like I am off my rocker. There was many a day when I thought I was. I can assure you I am as sane as the next guy—which might not be saying much. No need to fear Missy.

I have never invited another living soul into this room except for Frank who helped me set up the telescope. We can seal off the room to acclimate the scope to the outside air temperature and humidity before observations. I guess I never thought what this mess might look like."

"It's a little scary," Mina said still trying to make sense of what she was looking at. "What is all this and why bring me here?"

"My Frank," McKenzie began, holding back tears, "disappeared like your Jack. At the same gas station two decades ago. I get gas at Jacob's not so much for the convenience really. At first, I stopped by there hoping he might show up. After a few years, it just became habit and remembrance."

"What do you mean your husband disappeared like my husband?" Mina asked.

"I mean," McKenzie said, looking out the window, "Frank went into the gas station store to buy a Snickers Bar, a dad-burned Snickers Bar, while I filled the tank. He never came out. When I finally went in to look for him, he was gone. Unlike with you, however, the car was still there. I have my theories, but I don't know."

So," Mina asked, trying to connect McKenzie's story to her own, "what is all this stuff?"

"Research," McKenzie said. "I think I know a little bit about the what and how, and maybe the why of your Jack's separation from you."

"You have a theory, or you know?" Mina asked.

"It's more than a theory, Missy," McKenzie said. "I have proof of some of it. Now that you have seen this let's go back downstairs where it's comfortable, and I will tell you the whole story. We've got no time to lose, but we've got tonight."

CHAPTER 7
COCHRAN

COCHRAN FELT SORRY FOR THE young lady and found it interesting that she had connected with the recluse McKenzie. McKenzie wore ranch clothes like a man, cowboy hat and boots included, but she was a looker in her day. Cochran had first met McKenzie as a rookie cop when he had traveled to her ranch to follow-up on a report of a missing person. "That would've been 1993 or 94," Cochran reminded himself out loud as he sat down to his work computer. "The old Karas lady, McKenzie Karas," he added as he began to type. He loved this part of his job, and it was much easier with the digitization of all the documents that used to be filed in shoe boxes. He leaned back in his chair and let the computer do the work.

"Frank Karas, age thirty-two, new owner of the Sky Trails Ranch, disappears says wife of six years," Cochran skimmed the digital document. He started to remember the details. 'The official verdict on the case was the guy ran off, leaving his wife with a failing ranch. McKenzie Karas proved the old-timers wrong and made the ranch a success. She never gave up on her husband's return.' Cochran chuckled as he read the investigating officer's postscript. "Mrs. Karas suggested her husband vanished into thin air at the gas station near the intersection of Interstate 80 and Hunt Road. She said "he was there and then he wasn't." I asked if she was suggesting aliens abducted him, trying to get a fix on her mental veracity. She chewed me out for several minutes for making fun of tragedy. Her explanation of his disappearance was something to do with space-time and alternate realities. I never understood her, but research did uncover that she was a Stanford University graduate with a master's degree in astrophysics. One of the reasons for their move to Wyoming was to build a private observatory, telescope and all. Something about no light pollution. Mrs. Karas seems to be of sound mind and was never a suspect as she was in the company of others at the time of his disappearance."

Cochran did a Google search for the words "space-time," a capability the original investigating officer didn't have at his disposal twenty years ago. Cochran had trouble keeping the explanation clear as he read phrases like "fourth dimension," "special relativity," and "time travel." He had no idea that the reference to time travel had little to do with space-time except that it was touched on briefly in the 1895 novel *The Time Machine*, by H. G. Wells.

"Time travel?" Cochran repeated out loud the next morning. He could not get this thought out of his head. As he ate another tasteless and boring breakfast sandwich in his car in the parking lot of the local sandwich shop, he decided to drive out the McKenzie place. This is just too odd to not check it out. If nothing else he could talk to Ms. Gamble again. Something about her story just didn't add up. He finished his sandwich and drove out to McKenzie's ranch, wondering for the millionth time why people found this solitary life style so appealing. He had grown up here, but always felt like a fish out of water.

McKenzie heard the patrol car before she could see it. When she saw it was the police she got excited, hoping it was bringing news of Mina's husband. When Cochran got out of the patrol car, she went on alert. Cochran was not a bad person and did his job, but it was obvious to McKenzie that over the years the air had gone out of his balloon. He now only did what was required and had the backbone of a slug. McKenzie stepped out on the porch before he could knock on the door.

"Hey McKenzie, Cochran said. "Sorry to bother you if you have chores to do. Before I turn the case of the disappearing husband over to federal authorities," he explained quickly, "I wanted to make sure I got my facts lined up. Do you know where I can find Mrs. Gamble? Did she take my advice and stay in contact with you?"

"She's here," McKenzie said disappointed that he wasn't bringing any new information. If she was honest with herself, she was also more convinced and excited that what had happened to Frank also happened to Mina and Jack. And that left a tiny dot of hope that she would be able to get to the bottom of where her Frank is, or was.

"Can I talk to her?" Cochran asked. "It won't take but a few minutes. Sorry, I'm not bringing some good news."

McKenzie was surprised at Cochran's perceptive insight. He usually filled the squares and did the minimal amount of work required to get the job done. "She might still be sleeping. We had a long talk last night. I can't stay in bed, no matter how little sleep I get. This has been tough on her, and she doesn't realize how really exhausted she is. Can you come back this afternoon?"

"I've got to make my report McKenzie," Cochran explained. "You know those Feds, well maybe you don't. They would first skewer me for not contacting them as soon as the legal code requires. I don't need that hassle and the accompanying paperwork. Besides, the sooner they are on the case, the sooner they might solve this problem for your friend."

"Fine," McKenzie said, not sure she liked this new and improved Cochran. "You can park yourself on the porch, and I will go get her." McKenzie went inside and ascended the stairs and gently knocked on Mina's bedroom door.

"I'm awake," Mina's voice said from inside the room. "You can come in."

"Morning Mina," McKenzie said, noticing Mina was sitting up in bed reading one of McKenzie's files of notes. "Not sure how useful that will be, but glad you are reading it. The police are downstairs. No new info, but he says he has to talk with you again before bringing in the federal authorities. Are you ready for that?"

"Sure," Mina said. "You about convinced me last night, but I still want to look up every road of possibilities. I can be dressed and downstairs in five minutes."

"Okay," McKenzie said. "It might be hard reliving this again." She turned to go, but when she was about to close the door, she turned and added, "I wouldn't mention my theories if I were you. Nothing to hide, mind you, but they will think you are a nut, and it won't help. Believe me, I've got the t-shirt for that."

"I'll be right down," Mina said. She wanted to run McKenzie's theories by someone else if for no other reason than to see another person's reactions. Mina had not yet been able to take the leap into the crazy idea of parallel universes. "A fascinating idea for particle physics," Mina had said last night, "but we are talking about people here, and a gas station in the middle of nowhere as universe central. That is just too much to digest."

"Yes, it is," McKenzie had said. "Storytelling is the universal balm. I have wondered, in the silence of the night, when I have felt the most alone and things seemed the worst, whether I was just telling myself a story. With all my heart I want to believe

Frank didn't abandon me. But with all my heart I want him back, and that is not enough to make it so. Maybe what I believe about Frank isn't so either. I am not telling you this for me, Missy. I am warning you that this all could really be a story."

As Mina walked down the stairs, she could hear the police officer talking. "You know McKenzie, I looked back at your case, the disappearance of your husband twenty-two years ago. This case has a lot of similarities. That's kind of odd isn't it?"

Mina walked into the room and held out her hand. "Good morning officer, nice of you to come all the way out here. McKenzie said you didn't come with any updates."

"Sorry, Mam," Cochran said. "I wish I did have something new to share with you. But in a way, I do have some news, for you." Cochran paused, looked at McKenzie, and then back at Mina. "Did McKenzie tell you her husband disappeared from the same gas station about twenty-two years ago?" He watched for a reaction from either one of them. Nothing. So McKenzie had already spilled those beans. Interesting.

"I'm sorry," Mina said. "I thought you wanted to talk to me about Jack's disappearance." She was upset that this policeman was being so insensitive and apparently trying to get her reaction. "Are you suggesting there is a connection? Am I on trial here? Do I need to get a lawyer?"

"You can always get a lawyer, Mam," Cochran said. "All of that will be up to the Feds. Sorry for my insensitivities. You aren't a suspect, yet. Just doing my job and I am a little out of my league here. I can handle a bar fight, or a drunk trying to rob the dollar store, but we don't get many disappearances. Not enough people here for that I guess."

"So what would you like to know," Mina asked.

"Here is a written report of your story," Cochran said as he handed a stapled group of papers to Mina. "If you were under any suspicion I would ask you to recount it again orally, but you're not, and I don't want to have to put you through that again. Could you let me know if there is anything I should add or edit?"

Mina began to read the type-written notes. She heard Cochran ask for a glass of water from McKenzie, but kept reading. Then she felt the officer's hand on her knee.

"The thing is, Mina," Cochran began in a hushed voice, and Mina looked up to see they were alone. "I know you are hiding something. This little conversation is outside of the report and will stay that way if you cooperate with me. I'm not a bad guy, and I really want to help you, but you have to help me and tell me everything."

"Get your hand off of me, please," Mina said. "I have told you everything I know and everything I don't know for sure but believe. I am not sure what you are getting at, but you already have my full cooperation."

Cochran's hand was still on Mina's knee. Something in him snapped. Suddenly his whole life here in this wilderness lost all meaning. He squeezed harder. "Right," he said. "You know, McKenzie shared some really out of the box ideas with the investigating officer when her husband disappeared. It is either an amazing coincidence that you two connected, or there is something else going on here, and I want to be a part of it. Either let me in, or I will force my way in." He emphasized the last sentence with an extra hard squeeze that brought tears to Mina's eyes. Then he let go.

Mina wanted to yell at this gruesome man, but stood up and threw the report back at him. "You have done your job, now get out of here."

"I will leave when I have completed my sworn duties to uphold the peace," Cochran said with a smile. McKenzie walked back into the room with a glass of water.

"Officer Cochran," McKenzie interjected, "it looks like Mina is upset having to go through this again, as I warned you. Do you have anything else you need to do, or could we do it later?"

"Thanks for the water McKenzie," Cochran said. "Mina was just trying to remember if there was anything else she wanted to add to the report." Cochran took a drink of the water. "You have good water here McKenzie. Anything you would like to add to these events?"

"What events?" McKenzie asked. "I wasn't there."

"Of course you were," Cochran said. "You were there twenty-two years ago, and you were at the pump when Ms. Gamble here reached out to you. Did you know she was going to be there? Did you know what was going on, even if Mina Gamble didn't?"

"Cochran, you have known me for over two decades," McKenzie said, losing her temper. "In all that time, have I ever given you a reason to doubt me? What is going on in that head of yours? What do you think I would try to hide?"

Cochran smiled and took another sip of his water. "That's exactly it, McKenzie. I do believe you. I believe what you tried to tell the investigator all those years ago, about alternate universes and space-time. I'm on your side. And I want to help young Mina here find her beau. So what can you tell me?" He took another small sip of water, reminding them that he could sit there all day if need be.

"I was a distraught young woman back then," McKenzie began. "I went to my comfort zone. My education and my head were in the stars, and so I tried to take my heart there too. That is where I retreated. You need to keep your search closer to earth and find this lady's husband. My Frank is long gone, and that's that. Alternate universes. Are you nuts Cochran?"

Cochran wasn't sure where to go with this now. McKenzie did have a point. It's been two decades, and here she still was, eking out a living on a ranch in the frozen north. If she actually could travel in time, why would she be here? But he didn't want to give up on his possible ticket out of this Interstate 80 rest stop. He stood and smiled confidently at both women. "Maybe you're right McKenzie. This is all so odd that I am grasping at straws and finding answers where there are none. You ladies have a nice day, and I will let you know if I hear anything." He turned to Mina and said, "I hope this doesn't bruise…, our relationship."

He left the house sure of two things. He was not going to forward this to the Feds for another couple days, and these ladies were hiding something. McKenzie had not convinced him. He knew from rumors around town that McKenzie had not given up on connecting with her husband in another reality—whatever that meant. Certainly, his ex, Katy, was living in another reality. Unlike Katy, McKenzie was anything but a person that would run and hide when times go tough. Old timers had counted her out many times, but she had proved them wrong. She was a respected rancher and one that people would turn to if they were on tough times. Retreating to science fiction did not fit at all in McKenzie's playbook.

He would have to figure out a way to keep an eye on her and her new time travelin' sidekick Mina. He had a workable plan constructed by the time he walked into the police station. His first call was to shake the bushes a little with a phone call to the missing husband's mother with a number on the missing vehicle's paperwork. "Another reason to never co-sign for a loan," Cochran chuckled.

CHAPTER 8
COCHRAN

Officer Cochran watched Jack leave the police station for the second time today. The guy seemed like a reasonable person, but his story just didn't add up. The conversation with Jack's mother was more than strange. It also tickled a memory from years ago. Cochran had been a rookie cop, called out to support an investigation of a missing person. "That would've been 1993 or 94," Cochran reminded himself out loud as he sat down to his work computer. "The old Karas lady, McKenzie Karas," he added as he began to type. Cochran had access to all open and closed cases back to 1972. Long gone were the days of sorting through shoe boxes for dead case information. He leaned back in his chair as the case populated his screen.

"Frank Karas, age thirty-two, new owner of the Sky Trails Ranch, disappears says wife of six years," Cochran read as he scanned the digital document. It was coming back to him. 'The official verdict on the case was the guy ran off, leaving his wife with a failing ranch. McKenzie Karas proved the old-timers wrong and made the ranch a success. She never gave up on her husband's return.' Cochran leaned forward again at the investigating officer's postscript. "Mrs. Karas suggested her husband vanished into thin air at the gas station near the intersection of Interstate 80 and Hunt Road. She said "he was there and then he wasn't." I asked if she was suggesting aliens abducted him, trying to get a fix on her mental veracity. She chewed me out for several minutes for making fun of tragedy. Her explanation of his disappearance was something to do with space-time and alternate realities. I never understood her, but research did uncover that she was a Stanford University graduate with a master's degree in astrophysics. One of the reasons for their move to Wyoming was to build a private observatory, telescope and all. Something about no light pollution. Mrs. Karas seems to be of sound mind and was never a suspect as she was in the company of others at the time of his disappearance."

Cochran did a Google search for the words space-time, a capability the original investigating officer didn't have at his disposal twenty years ago. Cochran's head began to hurt almost immediately as he read phrases like "fourth dimension," "special relativity," and "time travel." He had no idea that the reference to time travel had little to do with space-time except that it was touched on briefly in the 1895 novel *The Time Machine*, by H. G. Wells.

A junior officer reported, just before Cochran was leaving for home. "Sir, here is the routine report on the disappeared person. It appears they each have a significant life insurance policy on each other. $250k." He tossed the report on his desk, thinking, 'I wish someone thought I was worth a quarter of a million dollars.'

"Time travel?" Cochran asked himself out loud. He didn't believe in all that science fiction stuff and thought no more about it until he was driving home that evening. Like most every day Cochran took 3rd Street south out of town. As 3rd Street became Highway 287, he passed the Cavalryman Steakhouse on the left and the New Life Assembly Church and the cement company beyond on the right. As he approached the Laramie Rivers Conservation building, he turned left and then left again onto Graham Road. This evening a small herd of antelope was crossing the gravel road, and he had to slow down, simultaneously bringing him out of his habit induced stupor. He realized he was almost home and had not even realized it. Not one for deep thought, Cochran pulled into his dirt driveway, parked, and stared at his empty single –wide mobile home. Another night of television, a frozen dinner, and a couple beers.

"I drove home without even thinking about it. It's like that time didn't exist. I was at the station, and now I'm here. Nothing in between. My body and my car physically traveled here, but I don't remember it. I was on commute anesthesia. Those 10 minutes will never exist for me. I don't remember what I did last night either, but I know what I did. Nothing. The last night I remember was the day Katy left me for that Roustabout. I'm sure she is sick of the oilfield life, but she has never even contacted me or tried to come home. Well, curse her and curse this stinking life." Cochran got out of his car and entered his house, ready for another mind-numbing night of *Bones*, *Law & Order*, and *Quantico*. Somewhere in the middle of a Priyanka Chopra scene, Cochran fell asleep. He dreamed of a bigger life as a lead detective in the big city, Los Angeles, New York, Chicago, Dallas; his mind never clearly identified it. He woke up about two in the morning. He felt alive. His heart was beating fast, and he could taste the air he was breathing. Until he opened his eyes. Then he was alone again, in his little box off a dirt road, in a tiny town in the middle of nowhere. Some people loved the wild open spaces of this part of the country. Big sky, crisp wind, nature in its prime. This place demanded the best of those who chose to live here. Cochran hated it, and he knew it was bringing out the worst in him, but he was done fighting those impulses.

"What is it McKenzie Karas is hiding?" Cochran asked the blank wall that used to display his and Katy's wedding picture. "Is there any connection between the Gamble lady's disappearance and McKenzie's husband's disappearance? Is there something I can use to get me out of this place? Blackmail maybe? Time travel? Right, time travel," he said with a scoffing laugh. "That would be something. I could start over as a younger guy. Maybe save my marriage? Forget Katy. I deserve a big city girl, along with a big city paycheck and a place looking out over the city that fears me and respects me. What would I do if I could actually travel in time? I could make a boatload of money and not even have to work. Now that would be nice." Cochran drifted back to sleep with a smile on his face for the first time in over a year. Tomorrow would be a new day, and he would put his talents to work for himself for once.

The next day, after checking in at the station, he drove out to McKenzie's place. He half hoped she wasn't at home so he could do some poking around. He found her walking from the barn when he drove up. "Morning McKenzie," he said as he stepped out of his patrol car.

"Morning. What brings you all the way out here?" McKenzie asked.

"We've got a case of a disappearing spouse," Cochran began. "Disappeared yesterday from Jacob's gas station over on Interstate 80."

"And what's that got to do with me?" McKenzie asked.

"It just sounds a lot like your case, and I thought I would ask you a few questions," Cochran said.

"That's really stretching things," McKenzie said suddenly on alert. "My husband Frank went missing over twenty years ago. You think some stalker is back to nab another person?" McKenzie tried to rustle up a laugh, but all that came out sounded like she was clearing her throat.

"Just wondering if any similarities would lead me anywhere, umm, profitable," Cochran said. "You know I was a junior officer when Frank disappeared. Something about that case feels a lot like this one."

"Cochran, you have known me for over two decades," McKenzie said, losing her temper. "In all that time, have I ever given you a reason to doubt me? What is going on in that head of yours? What do you think I would try to hide?"

Cochran smiled and kicked at a pebble on the ground. "That's exactly it, McKenzie. I do believe you. I believe what you tried to tell the investigator all those years ago, about alternate universes and space-time. I'm on your side. And I want to help this young man get his wife back. So what can you tell me?" He leaned back on his patrol car, reminding McKenzie that he could hang around all day if need be.

"I was a distraught young woman back then," McKenzie began. "I went to my comfort zone. My education and my head were in the stars, and so I tried to take my heart there too. That is where I retreated. You need to keep your search closer to earth and find this man's wife. My Frank is long gone, and that's that. Alternate universes. Are you nuts Cochran?"

Cochran wasn't sure where to go with this now. McKenzie did have a point. It's been twenty-two years and here she still was, eking out a living on a ranch in the frozen north. If she really could travel in time, why would she be here? But he didn't want to give up on his possible ticket out of this Interstate 80 rest stop. He stood and smiled confidently at this rugged woman. He was not going to be able to scare her or bluff her. "Maybe you're right McKenzie. This is all so odd that I am grasping at straws and finding answers where there are none. You have a nice day, and I will let you know if I hear anything." He turned to go and then turned back and said, "If you hear anything, or think of anything, you'll let me know won't you?"

"Of course," McKenzie said. "You have a safe drive back to town now."

He drove out of the ranch yard sure of two things. He was not going to forward this to the Feds for another couple days, and McKenzie knew something, even if she didn't at this moment realize it. She had not convinced him. He knew from rumors around town that McKenzie had not given up on connecting with her husband in another reality—whatever that meant. Certainly, his ex, Katy, was living in another reality. Unlike Katy, McKenzie was anything but a person that would run and hide when times go tough. Old timers had counted her out many times, but she had proved them wrong. She was a respected rancher and one that people would turn to if they were on tough times. Retreating to science fiction did not fit at all in McKenzie's playbook.

CHAPTER 9
JACK

ACK WOKE TO A POUNDING on his door. This was the first time he had been shocked awake by noises this night. He would have to find a better place to stay in Laramie than the Wagon Wheel Inn. Loud drunks, fights, howling at the moon, all seemed to be part of the ambiance of this motel. He pulled himself out of bed and realized the sun was up. "Just a minute," he yelled at the door. "Give me a second to put some clothes on." 'I will also have to get some clothes today,' he reminded himself. He pulled on his pants and put on his shirt, not bothering to button it, and opened the door. The sunlight partially blinded him.

"Mr. Gamble?" the man asked in a stern voice.

"Yes, that's me," Jack replied.

"Could you collect your things and come with me please, sir?" the man said.

"What's going on?" Jack asked. "Who are you? Where are we going?"

"We met the other day. I'm Officer Cochran from the Laramie City Police. I need you to come with me."

"Do you have any news?" Jack asked, suddenly awake and interested.

"We can't talk here," Cochran said. "As you might have noticed, this motel has no sound insulation. People three doors down could hear us whisper. Please, get your things. You won't be staying at this motel any longer."

Jack quickly completed getting dressed and put his new tooth brush and disposable razor in the plastic bag in which it was given to him by the motel clerk the night before and he left the room in anticipation of good news.

"We have a city rule that no one but a uniformed officer can ride in the front of a patrol car," Cochran explained. "Some might think we are using patrol cars for personal interests. Sorry you will have to ride in the back."

Still trying to wake up, Jack complied without a word. It wasn't until he was seated in the back of the patrol car that he remembered riding in the front seat with the other officer who gave him a ride to the cell phone company yesterday. And Cochran himself had given Jack a ride from the gas station to the police headquarters from the front seat. It wasn't that he cared which seat he was in, but he knew something was up.

When Cochran was positioned in the driver's seat, he turned to look at Jack through the wire mesh that separated the front from the back seat. "Yes, I was blowing smoke with that explanation. I didn't want to make a big scene by the motel. In that I was being truthful. You can hear everything through the walls of that place. What say we go on a little drive? I will give you time to wake up."

Jack didn't reply even though he had a hundred questions. He sat back and looked out the window. 'Do they think I killed my wife, or had a hand in her disappearance? Could they have found her and she's dead and they want to break it to me someplace else? Maybe identify the body? Oh, I hope not. I'm not sure I could go on without her.'

They were driving away from Laramie, heading east. Jack knew that much. Cochran had put the sun visor down, but the light was still on the horizon and the visor didn't help much. Just a few miles out of town, Cochran exited I-80 onto another road, heading north. Jack let out a little laugh when he caught the road sign, Happy Jack Road.

Cochran looked at Jack through the rear view mirror and saw where Jack was looking. "Hey that is pretty good humor," Cochran said. "An omen, a warning, I don't know, but it is pretty funny." Cochran continued to drive for another few minutes before pulling over and parking. He turned to Jack and asked, "Happy?" And he laughed until Jack thought Cochran had gone mad.

"Okay," Jack said, "I give up. What in the world is going on and why are we out here in the middle of nowhere?"

"Don't get me wrong, Jack," Cochran said. "There are many great things about Laramie, but sometimes it feels like the middle of nowhere. This is more like the nowhere of nowhere. No one knows we are here, and no one would find you before a mountain lion of the cold would claim you. Over thirty miles that way to Cheyenne. Almost that long back to Laramie."

"Thanks for the geography lesson officer," Jack said. "Why are we here?"

"To have a private conversation and make some important decisions," Cochran said.

"I don't suppose we are out here so you could tell me you have found my wife?" Jack asked.

"I would say you are right, Jack," Cochran said. "But I think I know where your wife is." He paused and then added, "Got your attention didn't I."

"You're not making any sense. Where is she?" Jack asked.

"She is a time traveler, Jack, so she could be anywhere," Cochran said, aware this sounded nuts even to him. "And I want you to prove it to me, then we can both cash in. You get your wife back, and I get—I don't know, the winning team for next year's Super Bowl or who has the winning number for the California Lottery. I don't want to be a big bother. Just one or two wins and I will be out of your hair forever."

"You have got to be kidding me," Jack said. "You drove me all the way out here to talk about your science fiction fantasy. My wife is not a time traveler. I have not seen her since she disappeared. She has not come back. You have been watching too many movies."

"You haven't seen her, yet," Cochran replied. "It sounds a little crazy, but it happened before around here. When your wife returns, I will be part of the welcoming committee—either as your best friend or your worst nightmare."

Jack was utterly speechless. He just shook his head and looked out the window.

"So, I guess we aren't going to be best friends then," Cochran said. "Get out."

Jack swung back around to look at the crazy cop. "What?"

Cochran got out of the car, opened the back door and said, "Get out."

Jack got out of the car, trying to understand what was going on. As soon as he was out, Cochran grabbed Jack's shirt, pulled him away from the vehicle with his left hand and punched hard with his right fist into Jack's unprepared mid-section. Jack doubled over, trying to breathe and failing. He fell to the dirt and lay there in the fetal position.

"You see, Mr. Gamble, I don't need you, but I do admit it would be easier working with you than having you in the way. I am going to put a warrant out for your arrest when I get back to the station. You are a prime suspect in the murder of your wife. I discovered you have a life insurance policy on her for $250,000. We could have split that, like friends, but now you will not get any of it, and you won't be here when she returns, which I would've bet my half of the insurance money that she will do just that. You better get a move on." Cochran looked at his wrist watch. "It will only take me about forty-five minutes to get to the station. Maybe another twenty minutes to complete my paperwork. Ten minutes to go to your motel room and discover you are gone. So let's say an hour and a half from now, you will be a wanted man."

"Are you crazy?" Jack asked, almost screaming. "No, that isn't even a question. That is fact. You think my wife time travels. Are you certain she wasn't abducted by aliens? Or maybe she is a shapeshifter or became a vampire."

"Maybe," Cochran said. "You've still only got an hour and a half. I hope you make this chase more fun than me finding you here in a couple hours." Cochran got back in his patrol car and was about to drive off. Then he rolled down his window and added, "It feels nice out right now, but it gets cold out here at night. You don't even have a jacket." He drove off leaving Jack coughing in the dust.

Jack sat down on the road and put his head between his knees. "This cannot get any worse, or weirder. Where are you, Mina? I need you back. What makes this insane cop think she is time traveling? That is so absurd, right?" What wasn't ridiculous was he knew he would be a hunted man soon. Cochran wasn't bluffing. He wouldn't have gone to such trouble if he was. "So where do I go from here?" He knew the answer. Home. If Mina were to ever look for him, it would be where they met, fell in love, and started their life together. It wouldn't be in Minneapolis which was an unknown to both of them. It wouldn't be here in Wyoming, assuming Mina hadn't been kidnapped. He started walking down the road he came from. He knew he was headed west. What he needed to find fast was the highway and a friendly trucker. He started to jog now that he had a direction and the beginning of a plan.

Fifteen minutes later Jack was tired and sweating. When he stopped to walk he got cold. 'This was not much of a plan,' he thought. As the dirt road turned south, he could hear the highway to his right. He decided to cut across the land to save some time. He reached what he was pretty sure was I-80 he was exhausted. He was surprised by the amount of traffic on the highway for early in the morning. He stuck out his hand with his thumb up. Just as he was starting to shiver, a semi-truck pulled over and picked him up. He climbed inside and said "Thanks."

"Where you heading?" the truck driver asked.

Jack was surprised the driver didn't care what he was doing out in the middle of nowhere without a jacket or anything else. "West," was all Jack said. He had decided over the past half hour that he would offer a little information as possible, in case the police did start a manhunt for him. Leaning back in his seat as nonchalantly as possible, Jack passed through Laramie. Twenty minutes later he saw the sign for Jacobs Quick Stop Gas. He knew that he might be a wanted man in another twenty minutes, maybe already, but he made a quick decision. "Can you drop me off here?"

The truck driver obliged, and as Jack watched the truck pull back onto the highway, he almost waved for the truck to stop so he could get back in, to safety. Instead, Jack watched the truck drive off and then he walked through the underpass to Jacob's gas station. He went inside and asked the young guy who hid mostly under a baseball cap and tilted head, like he was looking for something on the floor, for a piece of paper and a pen. 'The guy must be a project who works for some kindly old man named Jacob,' Jack thought. 'Probably hard to find good work out here in the middle of nowhere,' Jack added to his assessment of Jacob's gas station help.

Jack wrote out a note for Mina, paid cash for a small bag of Cheetos, opened the bag and put the note in it and placed it on the top of the gas pump they had used. Jack put a rock on the edge of the bag to keep it from blowing away. He thought about waiting for someone here that was heading west that he could ask for a ride. No big rig trucks stopped here, and most people it appeared were families with full cars. He walked back out to the interstate and stuck his thumb out once again. He had to get out of the local area and heading west, back to the known was better than heading east. He knew now he might never get to his new job in Minneapolis. That was the farthest care from his mind.

As he reached the interstate, Cochran's threats were in the forefront of his thoughts again. Jack had walked maybe a quarter of a mile down the highway with his thumb out, wondering if the next car that came along would be Cochran, when a classic old pickup pulled over.

"Want a lift?" the driver asked. "Where you headed?"

"California," Jack said as he hopped in, and so grateful he could give the young man a hug. The driver looked a little familiar, but when Jack looked at his eyes, he was sure he had not met him before. "My name's Jack."

"You're in luck," the driver said. "I'm making a delivery to Reno that's got to be there tomorrow. Quick dinner and a fill-up in Ogden, Utah and then Reno for breakfast. It will be an uncomfortable night, but you can get a little sleep if you want. I'm not much of a talker." The driver never offered his name.

They drove in silence, with Jack trying to sort out a plan once he got to California. At one point in the night, Jack was startled awake by the driver swerving. "Sorry," the driver said. "You can never tell when those mule deer will decide to cross the road. You doing okay?"

"Great, thanks," Jack said. "And thanks for dinner. I have never been to Ogden. Looked like a beautiful place right up against those mountains.

"Too many people, I think," was all the driver said. Jack tried to get back to sleep, but his mind kept going back to Mina. Where was she? Was she alright? Could he get in contact with her? Was going to California the right thing to do?

They arrived in Reno, just as the driver said, in time for breakfast. They ate at the Daughter's Café, set up in an old Victorian house. "Nice place," Jack offered. "You must have lived here once. This isn't a place you would just stumble upon."

"I've spent some time in Reno, before Laramie," the driver said. "No family. There's always work here. The Greyhound bus depot is only a block from here. You can catch the next ride to wherever in California for next to nothing. $25 or less. You okay with cash?"

"I'm good," Jack said. "Thanks to you covering my meals, that is. I still have my credit cards too." He didn't explain to this kind man that he didn't want to use them because he was afraid it would alert the police to his location. Jack had a thought. "Thank you for the ride. I appreciate it more than you know. I have been so wrapped up with my own worries. Are you doing alright yourself?"

"I'm good," the driver said with a smile that broke new creases in his face. "Thanks for asking."

"I never got your name," Jack said.

"Not necessary," the driver said. "Listen, Jack, I know you are running from something. You aren't the first person I have picked up with a load on his shoulders. I'm happy I could help. I just want you to know that the world outside that door is full of answers," the driver said as he pointed to the restaurant exit. "If you are willing to carry the burden of uncertainty, that is. Did you know there are 63,360 inches in 1 mile? Once I figured the circumference of the tires on a tow truck I used to have, at around 100 inches. That means the tire makes about 640 revolutions per mile. I drove about 900 miles today. I'm not all that good at math on the spot, but I know that is over one million revolutions those tires are going to between this trip and my return. That's a lot of bumps, some rocks, maybe a few sharp nails or other things that could damage the tire, or even puncture it. But it is also a lot of touch, with smooth stretches and some mighty fine scenery. Keep your feet on the road and you will get to your destination, and you will find whatever it is you are looking for. You take care now."

"Thanks," Jack said. "That's pretty deep for, umm, what I was ready for."

"Pretty thick for a delivery driver, you mean?" the driver asked with a second smile. "Truckers, and wannabe truckers like me, might be the Walt Whitmans and Mortimer Adlers of our age. I listen to or read a book about every three or four days. I have plenty of time to think. And I keep a journal so I can record those thoughts. But don't think about that. Think about what I said. Keep your feet on the ground and be grateful for the uncertainty."

Jack watched the driver turn to leave and then turn back to him. He said, "One more thing Jack." The friendly guy with no name pulled out a piece of paper and an open bag of Cheetos and handed them to Jack. "I am just guessing, but I think you might need this. It's authentic. If I am wrong just toss it. I didn't read the note, but I know another guy did. A Laramie police officer named Cochran, so watch yourself."

Jack was speechless and didn't even move his hand that held the note until the mystery man disappeared down the road.

* * *

An hour after Jack had left his gas station, Officer Cochran showed up at Jacob's Gas Station. In California, where Jack was from, a search warrant is required to track a cell phone. There is no privacy protection like that in Wyoming. Cochran had been watching Jack's every move and was surprised he had stopped here, what with the threats he had leveled on Jack. Instead of going back to the police station, Cochran had gone to the Verizon store Jack had used. Since Cochran had Jack's number from the police report, Cochran was able to obtain the phone's IMEI, the MCC (Mobile Country Code), MNC (Mobile Network Code), LAC (Location Area Code) and CellId in which a particular SIM is present. Using one of several open source applications, Cochran was using Opencellid, he could see which tower Jack was near. In a congested area, tracking would prove more difficult because there would be so many towers Jack's phone might use. Here in Wyoming, it was much easier as there were so few towers and none were over-used, thus shifting its workload to another convenient tower.

Cochran walked around the gas station, talked to the new employee, who couldn't confirm Jack had been there as he had been called in on the spur of the moment. "Jacob probably got sick and tired of all the people and decided to take the afternoon to do some fishing. That's good with me. I get time and a half when he calls me in like this." Cochran was hardly listening. He walked out to the pumps. He noticed the Cheetos bag on top of the pump but didn't bother with it. His mind was thinking about his next move. Cochran was going to take some emergency vacation to visit a sick relative in whatever direction Jack traveled. It appeared California was where Jack was going.

Just before leaving, Cochran shifted back to the present and noticed again the Cheetos bag being held in place by a rock. That was odd. Normally he would check it out to see if drugs were being left suing this mode. He grabbed the bag and quickly discovered the note. He read it, smiled, and then placed the bag with the note back on the pump. He decided he wasn't in that big of a hurry to start his vacation. He parked his car off the access road to the west of the gas station, far enough away from the station that he could watch the comings and goings without himself being easily noticed.

CHAPTER 10
MINA

McKENZIE LOOKED AT MINA FOR some sign of acceptance of what she had shared with her. They were both sitting on the couch, and Mina had been in listening mode for half an hour. "So, your husband disappeared at the same gas station, about twenty years ago. You kept this ranch going, hoping, expecting, he would return. He never did, so you started researching possible explanations. The conclusion you came up with was alternate universes?"

"Thanks for boiling down two decades to four statements and a question," McKenzie said. "Yep, you pretty much got it, though. Frank and I were both kind of nerdy. Some of my theories have some more solid backing from modern science. It's not like I am living in a fantasy world with dragons and fairies. And the timing that made Frank's departure, I call it an anadexterous passage, is not so hard to believe either."

"Anadexterous passage?" Mina asked.

"Right," McKenzie said. "Ana means many things, but I use it here as a prefix meaning about a person and dexterous means nimble with the body and mental agility. Together they mean nimble person passage. Of course ana also means "up" as in anadromous—the salmon who swim up-stream, traveling between two worlds, salt water and fresh water. Ana also means "again" as in repeat which is hopeful don't you think? And finally, ana means "back" as in anagram, a secret message that you and I are going to solve."

"So, back to the alternate universes theory," Mina said.

"You know, the organization that recently confirmed the reality of gravitational waves, LIGO, The Laser Interferometer Gravitational-Wave Observatory, I know, I would keep it simple and call it LIGO too; well, they completed the upgrades that would make the measurements of GWs possible, just two days before those waves reached earth. That was after two black holes danced around each other for millennia and finally consumed each other over a billion light-years ago. Missy, just so you understand what that means, one light year is about 10,000 earth years. And the results of those black holes collapsing into each other reached earth just two days after we were ready for their arrival." McKenzie stood and looked at the picture of her and Frank on the mantel. "Some say there is a thing called quantum fate. We stopped at that gas station at 4: 45. I remember looking at the dashboard clock, wondering if the gas station was open. I really had to use the restroom. I learned months later that the gravitational wave, GW150914, hit us at 4:50. If we had still been sitting in our car together, our reality would still be the same. A few steps apart and whoosh, we are in completely different realities. I call that particular GW the galactic weeper. Finders weepers… I don't know if Frank and I found it, or if it found us. If my theory is correct, I don't know which one of us is in the alternate universe, but I guess it doesn't matter. It used to matter. I wanted to know whether to be mad at myself for leaving Frank, or mad at Frank for leaving me. Now I'm not mad at anyone, just alone, and Missy, I don't want you to spend your life like this. I know a lot more than I knew twenty, even ten years ago."

"So I have to hang around that gas station waiting for another gravitational wave?" Mina asked.

"Heavens no," McKenzie said. "LIGO detected a much lighter GW about three months later, but after that, they haven't detected one in over a year. Maybe in the cosmic immensities, GWs are common, but in this case, it was just happenstance, bad luck. There may be other GWs, but they are so light, we can't measure them yet with our current state of capabilities. Who's to say another GW might not split realities in two again and there would be multiple Jacks trying to get back to you. Or even multiple Minas trying to reach multiple Jacks. Even with that concern, we have no way yet of telling when a wave will get here, only that it arrived when it did."

So, it was a gravitational wave that caused our split, but it's not what will get us back together?" Mina asked.

"Two things we need to focus on. The present and the future," McKenzie explained. First the present. I think you will be able to communicate with Jack. I say, I think, because first we have to communicate with Jack, in order to set up regular communications with Jack. And that is all assuming he is in an adjacent universe."

"I am a software geek and I am comfortable with all sorts of information technologies," Mina said, "but my head is swimming here. What are you talking about?"

"The stretch and squeezing of spacetime by gravitational waves both brings alternate realities closer together and then pulls them apart. Of course, this all happens in the fraction of a second. Have you ever had feelings, the nearly intangible sense, that you have a connection to somewhere you have never been?" McKenzie asked. Without waiting for an answer she continued. "Some languages even have words for that feeling. *Saudade* in

Portuguese, *Hiraeth* in Welch, *Dépaysement* in French, *Fernweh* in German, and *Toska* in Russian. They don't all mean exactly the same thing, but they all come close to expressing that sense of closeness that are five senses can't quite fathom. Sometimes those feelings are spiritual I am sure, whether you are a believer or not. And sometimes, maybe only a few times in a lifetime, those feelings might be from a parallel universe."

"McKenzie, you rescued me when I was all alone," Mina said. "If you are trying to rescue me now, with this explanation, I am still drowning and maybe going down for the third time."

"Sorry," McKenzie said. "I have thought about this a lot, but never explained it out loud to anyone. I guess my theory isn't all that clear outside my head. Let me back up a step. Let's call the space-time you and I are in right now the original. There is a line running from the San Francisco Bay area to Minneapolis, Minnesota through which a parallel universe intersects with us. The center and most powerful point of intersection along that line, actually, the center of that line, is right here in Laramie, Wyoming. Maybe Jacob's gas station is the apex of connectivity. Theoretically, you could set up a communications transfer point anywhere along that line."

"A transfer point?" Mina asked.

"None of your digital communications will work," McKenzie began. "But it is possible to pass along physical letters."

"Snail mail, Mina said, "across alternate universes?"

"Yes," McKenzie said. "The time frame is less than the blink of an eye, but it should work."

"Should work?" Mina asked. "You never tried it, or you have never gotten it to work?"

"I was able to connect with Frank, and then things just stopped," McKenzie said. "I don't even know if he is still alive. But the theory is scientifically sound."

"You haven't even convinced me there is such a thing as an alternate universe and that is where Jack is," Mina said. "I will withhold judgment on your trans-universal letter exchange theory."

"Just keep your mind open to the possibility, Mina. That's all I ask. It gets a little harder to believe as I get deep into the theory."

"Harder?" Mina asked. "Wow, this I can't wait to hear. This is where the fairies come in?"

"No," McKenzie said with a frown. "But just as magical."

"I'm sorry McKenzie," Mina said standing and walking over to her. "I guess I am joking as a defense mechanism. I don't want to start believing and be incredibly disappointed."

"Gravity goes through anything and everything, even black holes, did you know that?" McKenzie asked.

"No I didn't," Mina said.

"Gravitational waves leave some energy in black holes, but otherwise they pass though like its butter. It never encounters a door that can block out light waves or a lead wall that can block x-rays and radio waves. Nothing but eternal time can diminish gravitational waves. But gravity is one of the weakest forces in nature." McKenzie picked up the picture again from the mantel and stared at it until Mina began to be uncomfortable. Then she asked, "What other force of nature is like gravity?"

"Electromagnetic, and nuclear forces?" Mina guessed. "The four forces of physics."

"Impressive Missy," McKenzie said. And then on earth, we contend with yet other forces of nature, like the wind, the sun, rain, the oceans, temperature, and politics."

"Wait, what?" Mina asked. "Politics?"

"Just a joke to see if you were listening," McKenzie said, chuckling. "Science says it's the last fifty-five orbits of two black holes that create the gravitational waves we can now measure. That last tango between two galactic lovers before they fall into each other's arms. Their pull is so strong, that if I was sitting on the edge of even a small black hole, maybe one with the mass of a neutron star, my 150 lbs. here on earth would be 21,000,000,000,000 pounds there. And remember, gravity is by far the weakest of natural forces."

"So please, answer your question, what other force of nature is like gravity? I don't know," Mina said.

"Yes you do," McKenzie said. "I've seen it in your eyes. I can feel it in you. Think Missy, what is like what I just described?"

"For the love of Mike," Mina said, exasperated. "I don't know."

"Exactly," McKenzie said. "Say that again."

"I don't know," Mina said louder.

"No, no, Missy," McKenzie said, louder too.

"For the love of," Mina began, but she was cut off by McKenzie pouncing on her like a panther on a mouse.

"That's it," McKenzie said grabbing Mina's arms near her shoulders. "Love. Love is the force I am talking about. You can't deny it has a certain magic. And it has a power that has both launched and sank ships."

"But it's a feeling, not a force," Mina said in almost a whisper. "It motivates, it's a virtue, it is the why behind many actions, but it's not the how."

"Says who?" McKenzie asked.

"Well, I suppose love could be the basis for a law which then forces someone to comply," Mina said, trying to think. "That is hardly a force on its own."

"Ever hear of Pierre Teilhard de Chardin?" McKenzie asked. Without waiting she answered her own question. "He was a French philosopher and Jesuit priest who trained as a paleontologist and geologist. Sort of a Renaissance Man. Died ten years before I was born. Anyway, he suggested the following, "Someday, after mastering the winds, the waves, the tides, and gravity, we shall harness for God the energies of love, and then, for a second time in the history of the world, man will have discovered fire." That's flowery French for love is a force of nature."

"Sorry McKenzie, a beautiful statement, but hardly convincing for the scientist in me," Mina said.

"Let me tell you a story," McKenzie said. "I was born on the other side of the country from my grandmother. My mom and dad had moved to California from Kentucky in the early sixties. I was born in 1965. This was before the Internet, cell phones, or even cheap long-distance calls. Several hours after I was born, my dad calls his mom. He says, "Guess what, I've got great news." My grandmother says, "No, let me tell you." And she goes on to describe the entire event as if she had been there. The time on the clock, the device the doctor used to monitor my heartbeat through the birth canal, the concern the doctor had about that monitor not working correctly and decision to use forceps to expedite my birth, and many more particulars. My grandmother's only explanation was, "I just dreamed it. Congratulations on your new baby girl, son." Back in those days, we didn't know the gender of the baby until it was born. Did my grandmother just make a lucky guess? No way. Was she a fortune teller? Never. How did she do that? I have no explanation except the unifying power of love. Maybe that is a gift from God. Maybe love just is. I don't know for sure."

"That's a fascinating story, McKenzie," Mina said. "You were a lucky girl to have a grandmother like that. But that doesn't prove your fuzzy theory."

"It's more than a fuzzy theory, Mina," McKenzie said. "A little over a decade ago, the Nobel Prize in Physics was awarded jointly to David J. Gross, H. David Politzer, and Frank Wilczek, for discovering the strong interaction of particles as they separate. This strong interaction is the force that holds the nuclei of an atom together, for example. They developed the theory and the mathematical equations to show that Quarks are held together by a strong force which, unlike any other force in the universe, gets stronger as the quarks get farther apart. They called this phenomenon Asymptotic Freedom. I would have called it Paradoxical Freedom, but no one asked me. Even earlier, Einstein noted that photons, that is, light particles, travel together instead of acting randomly as quantum physics would suggest. And, by the way, that led to the discovery of the laser." McKenzie smiled at the glassy look on Mina's face. "Hold on, Missy, I'm getting there."

Just like the recent proof of gravitational waves, there was a less publicized, but just as amazing and radical discovery by physicists in Hungary and at the University of California, Irvine. They were looking for dark protons as indicators of the dark matter that science says may make up eighty-five percent of all matter in the universe. Their experiments found a new force. A fifth fundamental force. They call their force carrying particle a protophobic X boson. Understanding this particle, and this possible fifth force could change how we understand the Universe because it appears to exist beyond time and space. The reason I am explaining all this to you is, it would also explain why we, humankind, have this desire to unite, even as we are being pulled apart. De Chardin expressed it this way, "If there were no real propensity to unite, even at a prodigiously rudimentary level, indeed in the molecule itself, it would be physically impossible for love to appear higher up in the 'hominized' or human form." I personally think love would still exist, but it is powerful to consider it exists even at the molecular or atom levels. So for Christians, what is the ultimate expression of love?"

"I don't know," Mina said, thinking. "Jesus Christ? Dying on the cross, atoning for everyone's sins?"

"Yes," McKenzie said. "Another example of Asymptotic Freedom. He unifies and brings together as others attack and kill him. How about Islam? The Prophet Mohamed is used as the excuse for terrorist actions when the pure religion is one of peace. How about Hinduism? The Bhagavad Gita, the "Song of God" is an epic argument persuading a warrior to engage in a battle, Krishna exhorting Arjuna to engage in a violent confrontation, yet this is the book Mahatma Gandhi used to fuel his non-violent fight and unify India, and for a time Pakistan. Krishna meant only that Arjuna should do his duty. Fighting, the Asymptotic to Gandhi, was nothing more than a metaphor for the inner struggle of human beings. His call to nonviolence, and eventual freedom, the urge to come together, was the precipitate of detachment. I could go on. The urge to connect isn't the Flower Power of the 1960s. It's a force that holds the universe together. It can't be observed with an electron microscope or the LIGO experiment, or the Hadron Collider. Like the Spanish philosopher, Miguel de Unamuno warned, when we dissect something to understand it, we kill it, we strangle the light out of it. As we examine the pieces, we say, "See, there is no light here. This is obviously a mistake." We cannot know the square root of the live ash tree, Unamuno reminds us. Equally, we can't understand love as a force until we surrender to it and leave it whole. Science, as it stands, has reached an impasse, the edge of a black hole of its own making, unless it meekly accepts all sensory experience, including divine authority, intuition, the spiritual, love, and the universal urge to connect."

"So in the midst of stars, planets, interstellar gas nebula, black holes, and whatever else, you want me to believe that love is what is holding it all together, even as the universe continues to expand?" Mina asked.

"You are looking at this with the wrong set of glasses," McKenzie said. "Have you ever seen an atom?"

"No, not personally," Mina said. "But someone has."

"Right," McKenzie said. "And you accept that on trust and your own understanding of nuclear science. Has anyone ever seen a quark? The answer is no. Some instruments can detect them when combined into hadrons. But we accept that they exist. Yet quantum physics suggests that observation not only disrupts measurements, but the act of observation actually defines location and specific attributes. When we observe we produce the results of the measurement. What I'm saying is, the observer creates the reality. We become creators of our own reality."

"Go on," Mina said.

"The universe is a mental construction, Mina," McKenzie said. "It's physical, but the physical is only real because of our observation and thought driven constructs."

"Mind over matter?" Mina asked. "We are just someone else's big science experiment? Or, who was it that said I think, therefore I am?"

"Cogito ergo sum," McKenzie said. "René Descartes. His thought was, if one were ever to doubt their existence, that very thought demands something to do that thinking, therefore they must exist. The modern quantum physicist would say, reality doesn't exist without an observer. I'm not pushing any of this. All I'm saying is, there is a force out there that isn't physical in the traditional sense of the word. The only way we can truly understand that force is to think in a different way.

CHAPTER 11
MCKENZIE

"**G**OD HAS NO PART IN this?" Mina asked. "Or do you think we are God? That we are the creators?"

"I think the universe is more mental than physical, and more spiritual than mental," McKenzie replied. "We are no more God than the guy who flips a light switch and thinks he created light and the electricity that powered it. But we do have our part to play. Science is slowly realizing that we are not just on the outside looking in, but we are on the inside and part of the equation. The German theoretical physicist, Max Planck, said something like, "Science cannot solve the ultimate mystery of nature because, in the last analysis, we ourselves are a part of the mystery that we are trying to solve." He said that about one hundred years ago. It was theory then. It's a quantum reality now."

"So, back to love as the binding force," Mina said. "Where does that leave me? I know that this universe binding theory isn't about me, but I just lost my husband, so it is about me, and that is pretty much the only thing I care about right now."

McKenzie smiled and was silent for a moment, staring at the picture of her and her husband. Then she said, "It is all about you, Mina, but only when you realize it isn't about you."

"Enough riddles, McKenzie," Mina said with much less frustration than she felt. "Either you have an answer, or you don't, but no more games."

"Fair enough," McKenzie said. "To harness the power of love, we have to let go of ourselves and focus on *the other*. By definition, *the other*, those who are not us, are different, almost alien. The history of humans is sadly about the other. Imperialism, colonialism, bigotry, xenophobia, nationalism, social classes, even social media and things like Facebook and Twitter, depend on *the other* to fuel their fire. We are back to the asymptotic freedom. You love your husband, don't you?"

"Yes, of course," Mina said.

"Then you have the power to connect with him, just like gravity can hold planets in orbit around their sun. This is going to sound a little like pixie dust, but you have to authentically believe and then let go of yourself, focus on Jack, and I will show you how to pull him close enough that you can communicate."

"Did you ever connect with Frank after he, um, was separated from you?" Mina asked.

"Yes, we connected, three times," McKenzie said. "Frank called our ability to connect the *hanker anchor*. He was the rancher, and I was along for the ride. In his universe, he was at this ranch and talked like a rancher."

"So what happened?" Mina asked.

"I don't know," McKenzie said. "We had a fourth connection planned, and he never showed. I don't know if I lost the ability to harness pragmatation, or if," McKenzie began as Mina cut her off.

"Pragmatation?" Mina asked.

"That's the word that I use for the fifth force, the word, for Frank's hanker anchor," McKenzie said. "Pragma is one of the six forms of love according to the Greeks. It's the mature love between a couple that makes an effort to give love rather than just receive it. "Tation" means "action or process." Thus the force I have been describing is a selfless love that is an active process. The name isn't all that important. That it either broke or something happened to Frank is the point. But it is worth trying with you and Jack, don't you think?"

"Just about anything is worth trying," Mina said.

McKenzie looked serious again, like she was about to continue her long explanation, but then she got a tender smile on her face and said, "Then let's get this show on the road. You feed the chickens, and I will go milk and feed the goats, Oh and don't forget to collect the eggs."

"That's getting the show on the road?" Mina asked.

"I run a ranch, Missy," McKenzie said. "We take care of the animals first, then our own agendas. Asymptotic Freedom."

Nearly an hour later McKenzie stepped back into the house. Mina stepped out of the kitchen where she had just finished washing up. "I don't like chickens," Mina said in greeting.

"Well, maybe tomorrow I will show you how to milk goats then," McKenzie said. "You ready to go for a ride?"

"Is this getting the show on the road or another chore?" Mina asked.

"Grab that paper and a pen," McKenzie said. "I will explain the rest on the way."

"So here is the plan," McKenzie began, and they bounced down the dirt road heading to the interstate highway. "You last were together at the gas pump at Jacob's place. That is where we will leave the message."

"The message?" Mina asked.

"The message that Jack will get from you," McKenzie said. "It will detail the places you will meet over the next month. The places have to be along the San Francisco to Minneapolis line, because, like I explained, that appears to be where your and Jack's time-space realities intersect. The middle and most powerful connection is, for some cockamamie cosmic confluence, Jacob's Gas Station."

"Well, if I can pass a note to him at the gas station, why not just meet there?" Mina asked. "And what do you mean by meeting? If we can meet, why can't one of us step to the other's side of the line?"

"Take it from me, you want to pick places that are semi-private, or at least different, random, but that also have a special connection between the two of you. Remember, it's love that is going to make this happen. The meetings will only last less than a second and you will be able to pass an inanimate object, a note, but only something you can grab and hold onto in that fraction of a second exchange."

"So I am back to third grade and passing notes to my crush, fast, so the teacher doesn't catch us." Mina surmised.

"That's about it," for now," McKenzie said. "You will need to be in the same place during an actual gravitational wave, to be able to cross the line, as you put it. The problem with that is, we only know how to measure a wave event, not predict one. For now, you will have to be patient and comfort yourself that you two were able to connect at all."

"You say that like it will for sure happen," Mina said. "How is Jack going to know to go to the gas station, to that gas pump? And is the timing critical? It sounds like it is less than a second?"

"No one should spend even a second in Jacob's bathrooms," McKenzie said, "but out at the pumps the time comes and goes. Leave the note on the pump, and there is a very real chance it will travel at the speed of love to the universe Jack is standing in. Is there something you can leave with the note? Something that will strengthen the note's ability to pragmatate?"

"You mean like my wedding ring or some other memorable item?" Mina asked.

"Something like that, but not something as valuable as your wedding ring," McKenzie said.

"How about a bag of Cheetos?" Mina said chuckling.

"If you are serious that is something that will connect with Jack," McKenzie said. "That might be helpful too because it would be something he would see and maybe want to look at."

"This is completely ridiculous," Mina said. "You want me to believe that love is a physical force and that Jack is in another universe. We are going to be able to connect, and a bag of Cheetos will help make that happen. Complete fantasy, no matter how much I want it to be true."

"Embrace the sheer audacity of the idea," McKenzie said. "I will admit, being able to act on the idea requires the faith of Job in the face of uncertainty and the naiveté of a young lover. You've got the second, now work on the first."

"Jack used to always say, reality is only a probability until we act," Mine said. "Let's go pass notes."

Mina listed five places and times in her note; five places of progressively higher meaning in their relationship. She added a brief explanation of McKenzie's theory so Jack could do his own research, and perhaps meet the McKenzie in his universe if there was one. She showed the note to McKenzie to make sure her explanation made sense. McKenzie liked the idea of Jack meeting her other self and wondered what she would think of this stranger driving up to her ranch with her own explanation.

Mina was shocked to see a bag of Cheetos sitting in the very spot she had planned to leave her note. She grabbed the bag and discovered there was a note attached. She almost dropped the note when she saw it had Jack's handwriting on it. She glanced around and couldn't see anything out the ordinary, and in particular, no Jack coming out of a hiding place. "Was this all just a big joke? Had he just taken off and this note his guilty pangs getting the best of him? No way," Mina said to the wind.

She carried the note back to McKenzie's vehicle. "A note, from Jack," Mina said, holding the crumpled paper up to show McKenzie. McKenzie gasped but said nothing. Mina opened the paper and read silently, then aloud.

Mina, if this note finds you, it will be because our love in bigger than the chasm that separates us. I can't tell you all the fears I have and how unexplainable your disappearance is. You went into the gas station and never came out. But you weren't there. I don't know what happened, but I want you to know I would never abandon you and I know you have not left me. Unfortunately, others think differently. The local police, in particularly a guy named Cochran, thinks we are time traveling and wants in on the action. He has actually framed me for your disappearance and possible murder. I am now on the run. He is probably attempting to follow me to see if you appear. So watch out for this sicko. I am on my way back to San Francisco, and I hope that is where you are. I am leaving this note in the crazy chance that you stop here looking for me. I love you and will find you. If you are in trouble, hold on, and we will figure this out. Love, Jack

"Oh, my," Mina began and couldn't finish her words. She broke down and began to sob with a pain that she thought should have killed her.

"There, there Missy," McKenzie said. "This is good news, you know."

"Good news?" Mina spat. "He was here, and now he isn't. He is on his way home, but not our home, at least not the home where I can reach him."

"But at least now you know he is alright," McKenzie said. "He didn't leave you. And he is on the right track, that you didn't leave him either, but that this all has something to do with time and space."

"But how can I contact him now?" Mina asked. "And he has the police after him? And,"

"And," McKenzie interrupted, "he has more faith in love than you do. His note to you crossed the chasm. It was in his hand in another reality, and now it is in your hand. Let's leave your note and let love do its part."

Mina left the note on top of the gas pump with a bag of Cheetos, both held down by a rock. They left the gas station because, according to McKenzie, "If we watch the note itself, it won't leave our universe. "Observation defines location. Quantum superposition is very shy. It's asymptotic freedom, Mina. Losers, keepers."

CHAPTER 12
COCHRAN

OFFICER COCHRAN WATCHED MCKENZIE, AND the Gamble girl drive away from Jacob's Gas Station. He had been following them since they left the ranch. He expected them to travel back to town. He wasn't sure what their game was, but he was certain something odd was happening, and it still pointed to time travel to him. He drove up to the pump where they had stood apparently discussing something. He looked in every direction. Nothing but the same dull, worn out landscape he had seen his whole adult life. He slammed his hand on the gas pump beside him. He turned his head away from the gas station to scream and saw a Cheetos bag. "That is odd," he said out loud. "A Cheetos bag being held in place by a rock."

He grabbed the bag, thinking drugs or drug money, but it was a real bag of unopened Cheetos. And a note. He opened the note and smiled. He read the locations, and he read Mina's explanation of alternate universes. He took a picture of the note with his phone and put it back on the pump just as he had found it.

"Yes," Cochran screamed, letting out all his frustration of a minute ago plus his feelings of vindication. "Sounds like some kind of time travel to me, you sorry sack of goat dung, McKenzie." He looked around once more and seeing nothing out of the ordinary, he got back in his car and drove back to his inconspicuous parking place to watch for the Gamble girl's husband to appear. "Would he just pop up? Would he appear with a car?"

Cochran waited all afternoon without ever taking his eyes off the gas station. Nothing happened, and although a few people stopped to get gas, no one reached for the bag of Cheetos.

In frustration, Cochran drove back to the pump to make sure the note and snack bag were still there. To his surprise, the note was gone and the bag of Cheetos was opened and half empty. "There was no way I missed someone messing with that bag, let alone taking the note. Something did happen, and right under my nose."

He thought about some of the words in the note he had a picture of. He got out his phone and looked at it again. He scanned down and read aloud, "*We all time travel we just don't realize it. Lose something and wonder why like we had forgotten or weren't paying attention when often we were actually in another place. Then when we try to find it, we travel back in time in our mind to recreate where the last time was that we were aware of having that object. Finding the object is often a kind of travel. Time is actually the only imagined thing. The travel is very common.*" His hands trembled. Had he witnessed time travel? Well, maybe by missing the visit, that proves that time travel exists. He had been in the present, but someone had obviously come and gone, and he hadn't seen it. What other explanation could there be?

Picking up his phone again, this time he made a call. He had an out of work drinking buddy that was just crazy enough to get involved in getting to the bottom of this. He asked his friend to go out to McKenzie's place and shake things up just a little. He would follow a while later and see what information the ladies might then be willing to share.

Paxton was not all that happy to hear from Cochran. Keeping the local cop on your friendly side seemed wise, however, so here he was driving up to the goat lady's place. He figured he would push her around a little like Cochran had asked. Once he saw a younger lady putting some things into the only vehicle on the property, he thought maybe he would stay a little longer and have some fun. He was only doing what the local law requested, right?

"McKenzie," Mina said reentering the house, "you have a visitor. A middle-aged guy who I don't think is from the police." Mina stayed inside while McKenzie stepped out onto the porch.

"Can I help you?" McKenzie asked, recognizing the guy as a local, but not being able to put a name to the face.

"I was just passing through and was wondering if I could borrow your facilities," the man said, continuing to approach.

McKenzie wished she had grabbed here shotgun before stepping outside. This was the most visitors she had had in a two-day period since moving to the ranch. "Right. Since when does a cowhand need modern facilities to take care of his needs. There's an outhouse on the south side of the barn, you're welcome to it."

Paxton reached the steps and said, "Now that you mention it, I did see a pretty little lady out here as I pulled up. I'd like to take her to the south side of the barn. But first I have a question. What do you know about leaving a note at Jacob's Gas Station?" He was to the top of the porch stairs and within reach of McKenzie.

"Time for you to leave," McKenzie said with force and no fear. "I will beat you to a pulp and feed you to my chickens if you come one step closer."

"My, aren't we feisty," Paxton said with a chuckle. "Answer my question, and I will be on my way. Play Betty Brickwall with me, and I will knock you down so hard the pieces can't be put back together. Now tell me about the note. Did you know it disappeared?"

McKenzie tried to hide her surprise. "Like I said, young man, it's time to git."

"Okay, if that's how you want it," Paxton said. He took a step closer, his tobacco-stained smile growing.

"That's far enough," Mina said stepping out the door with the shotgun in her hands. "Betty Brickwall just told you to go. Mind her, or I will, how did you say it? I will knock you down so hard the pieces can't be put back together."

"Aw, I was just joking," Paxton said, although his smile had shrunk to a straight line. I don't want to cause anyone a problem. Maybe you can tell me about the note."

"I don't know what you are talking about," Mina said. "One thing I can tell you is, this shotgun is a lot heavier than I imagined. At some point, I am just going to shoot because I don't want to hold it too much longer."

"Why don't you just lay it down then and we can all talk," Paxton said, trying to inch closer to McKenzie, so he could use her as a shield.

"That's it," Mina said, and a shell exploded at the feet of this slimy man. It made a mess of the porch floor and sent several large splinters into Paxton's lower legs. He screamed out, and McKenzie took the moment to grab the gun from Mina who was shaking now.

"A few little slivers aren't going to kill you," McKenzie said. "Now get going, or it will be buckshot in your legs with the other barrel." McKenzie poked at Paxton with the business end of the shotgun, and he began to limp down the stairs.

"This isn't the end of things, ladies," he yelled as he pulled himself into his car. "You opened the box, and there are people who want to peek inside." He drove off with jolting actions.

"Ha, ha," McKenzie laughed. "I think pushing down on the accelerator is more painful than walking. Now that is an odd thing. Do you think that half an excuse for a police officer Cochran put him up to this?"

"McKenzie, I am so sorry for messing up your porch floor," Mina said. "I was so afraid I was going to shoot him in a vital organ or something, I guess I aimed lower than I thought."

"You did perfect Missy," McKenzie said. "Now we need to get you on the road. That cowboy was right about one thing, someone is coming back, and we need you gone."

"One good thing," Mina said. "Did you catch what he said. The note was gone. The note was gone, McKenzie."

"Speaking of notes, you will need to practice note swaps," McKenzie said. It's one thing to describe it in a note and another thing to do it. She showed Mina how to hold a note and drop it while grabbing a hoped for note with the other hand. "Just like I had you explain to Jack, if you don't grab the note it isn't observed, and it doesn't stay in your universe."

Mina practiced the drop and grab until her hands and arms ached. They were driving back to Jacob's Gas Station, this time just for gas. From there McKenzie planned to drive Mina to Rock Springs where they would spend the night and Mina would catch the bus to San Francisco. McKenzie would have liked to drive her all the way, but with goats to milk and chickens to feed, she had to get back right away in the early morning.

Mina watched McKenzie go into the gas station store to purchase a few snacks. Mina was scared to death to go back in that building. She picked up the half consumed bag of Cheetos from on top of the pump and allowed herself a tiny smile for the first time since she walked into the station restroom just a few days ago. "Or was it a universe ago?" she asked the bag. "Time really has no place in the equation when the separation is this severe."

When you know that something has happened and you don't want to admit it, the mind offers some crazy alternatives. Mina thought she almost saw Jack walk out of the station store. "Jack," Mina said matter-of-factly, "just come out of the store and let's begin our lives again. Come on, just walk out that door." Not only didn't Jack appear, but neither did McKenzie. Mina took in a deep breath and walked up to the door. She could see inside. There was that Jacob guy, reading a paperback behind the counter. She couldn't see anyone else. She let out her breath and pulled the door open.

"Have you seen McKenzie?" Mina asked Jacob.

Jacob stared at her trying to remember where he had seen her before and how she might know McKenzie. "I haven't seen her in maybe three days," Jacob said. 'Didn't she stop for gas just before his fishing trip?' Jacob tried to remember. "You could drive out to her place if you know her."

"Look out there," Mina said almost losing her ability to speak. "That is McKenzie's vehicle. I just came here with her."

"Then, I don't know," Jacob said. "Maybe she walked around the back. She didn't come in here. I would have noticed. It has been dead all day."

"This is not happening," Mina said, now talking to herself. "I can't do this alone." Turning to Jacob, she asked, "What kind of a place do you run here? I mean do half of your customers disappear leaving their cars here for you to sell on some black market?"

"Lady," Jacob said, wondering if she was going to go ballistic in his store. "I don't know what you are talking about, but you need to calm down. No sense winding your watch so tight. You're going to break a spring." He was pretty sure she already had.

"Wind my watch too," she couldn't even finish her sentence. Mina stormed out of the store and walked to the interstate. For a moment as she walked past the pump where McKenzie's car was parked she considered taking it. 'If McKenzie was in another universe she wouldn't need her car her, right?' But Mina couldn't take it. Besides, that crazy cop would probably charge her with grand theft or something. No sooner did she get to the interstate and put her thumb up, then a van pulled up and a door popped open. She got to the vehicle before she even thought about any dangers. The driver was a harried mom with two children in the back seats.

"I couldn't just let another single lady stand there on the highway," the driver said. "Get in. I want to make it to Reno by tomorrow morning. Can you drive?"

At about the same time Mina jumped in the van, McKenzie stepped out of the restroom at the gas station. "Jacob, you ought to go to prison for letting those toilets become the epicenter of the next plague outbreak."

"McKenzie," Jacob said, "how did you get here? Some other lady was just in here asking for you."

"You knucklehead," McKenzie said. "Someone could rob you blind for how little you notice what happens at this station. I walked right past you, and unfortunately for me, I have a long drive ahead of me, and nature called. So did the lady go back out to my car?"

"I don't know," Jacob said. "She looked like she was going to come unglued and she left, almost in a run."

McKenzie shook her head and walked to her car. She couldn't see Mina anywhere. She drove around the back of the store and out to the interstate and back to the gas station. She parked by the store, and told Jacob to let Mina use his phone and call her if she showed back up. McKenzie only half believed Jacob would remember her request.

"That poor girl," McKenzie said as she headed home. "She must have thought I had abandoned her, of left the universe.

McKenzie had another thought as she pulled into her ranch yard. She smiled as she called to her complaining goats. "Quit your bellyaching. You were going to have to wait until tomorrow morning, but you got a reprieve."

Before she could even tend to her goats, Cochran drove into the yard. McKenzie saw that the cowboy that had visited earlier was in the seat next to him. McKenzie ran to the porch and grabbed the shotgun that she had leaned against the house near the front door.

She felt better with the shotgun cradled in her arm. The cowboy stayed in the squad car. Cochran got out and stomped straight up to McKenzie. She was surprised by his anger. He was not thinking straight.

"McKenzie," he shouted. "Let's drop the tough girl act. You and I both know you aren't going to shoot me. I want some answers, and I want them now. Not after we talk a few minutes and prance around like to fighting roosters. Start talking now, or I promise you this is your last day on earth."

"Talking about a prancing rooster," McKenzie said. "I'm not afraid of you Cochran. Now get off my property, or I will surprise us both and pull this trigger."

"Right," Cochran said. "Go ahead and shoot."

They both heard a click as McKenzie pulled the trigger. It startled Cochran but did not slow his advance. About the time he reached her, McKenzie had found the other trigger, mentally kicking herself for forgetting the first barrel had already been discharged. The second shot went off as Cochran grabbed the barrel and pulled it up and away from himself. The shot exploded harmlessly into the sky and other than a few barn sparrows being spooked, McKenzie saw it did no harm. Then she heard Cochran scream.

"Arrgh," Cochran yelled as the heat from the discharge warmed the barrel and Cochran's hand wrapped around it. He let go of the gun, and it dropped to the ground. With his other hand, he exchanged his pain with a slap of McKenzie's face.

McKenzie made no audible noise as she fell to the ground. He stood over her cussing and waving his hand in the air. McKenzie did not move. He stepped over her and entered the house. He tore the place apart looking for Mina. He sent Paxton to search the barn and other areas around the house. Paxton moved slowly, but he was thorough. They came up with nothing.

Cochran poured a pitcher of water on McKenzie who hadn't moved during their search. She still didn't move. Cochran felt for a pulse and confirmed she was still alive. "She won't be of any use to us for a while. I know where the Gamble girl was heading, so let's pack up and get moving. You up for a road trip?"

"If it means getting even with that young filly, then what are we waiting for?" Paxton spat.

CHAPTER 13
JACOB

TUESDAY
SEPTEMBER 15, 2015, 2:21 P.M.

THE FISHING HAD BEEN GOOD. It always was, even if he didn't catch anything. Jacob loved his day and a half on the North Fork of Cooper Creek with his dog Beau. He was grateful for the gas station, having inherited it from his uncle who had disappeared six years ago. It provided a more than comfortable income and it gave him a roof over his head and other necessities. It also felt like a prison most of the time. Nothing ever happened there. If it wasn't for the gas station, he admitted with a half-smile, he would never interact with others of the human family. He supposed in some way that was healthy, but he would have been just as happy he guessed to live in the mountains with his dog and never see another person.

When Jacob was alone fishing on a river, walking a trail through the Wind River Range, or sitting at a campfire anywhere out of town, it seemed like time didn't exist. There was not an hour to open the gas station or close it. He didn't have a lunch time. No clocks. No customers asking how long it would take to get to Denver or Salt Lake City. He was just there, in the open sky, with the breeze, the slow-moving stream, and the fish. There were more varieties of fish in the lakes, but the Brown Trout that battled the fly fishermen in the North Fork made his life worth living. The sun moved across the sky during the day and moon at night, but he could stand in the stream and not even notice the passing of time.

The casual observer and those who would say they knew Jacob were all wrong. He wasn't slow of thought or brutish as he appeared. That was mostly an act. He had a hard time with people and found early in life that the easiest way to not be bothered with sociality was to give people reasons to not make an effort to spend time with him. He didn't want to push people away and make them feel bad, so he made himself the target. Even the disgusting state of the bathrooms at his gas station was calculated to reduce human interaction with him. He didn't mind people buying gas or the few retail items he offered, but getting to know people and opening up even just a little of himself was as painful as taking his hunting knife and making a slice on his thigh.

He chuckled now and then, especially as he completed his end of month finances, at the thought that people hadn't figured out that he was running a very successful business, for someone who most assumed had no thought in his head. And they never even noticed that he always had a book in his hand. He read one or two books a week, usually mixing both fiction, non-fiction, and religion—some of which he placed in the fiction category and most he believed to be non-fiction. Jacob didn't have a formal college education. He barely made it through high school. He did have an Internet connection and had toyed with the idea of taking some online classes, but even that took interaction with people to get the ball rolling. He loved being able to buy books through Amazon and other booksellers. He hadn't shifted to an electronic reading device like a Nook or Kindle. He preferred the tactile nature of printed books. Besides, he could go into the mountains for a full week with a few books without a worry of a battery going dead. Outside of his dog, fishing, and camping, books and observing people from a distance were his only other passions.

Sitting back in his chair at the gas station, his mind wandered to the stream he most recently fished. "If the stream was flowing west to east at six miles per hour, then it was really traveling at 736 miles per hour because the speed of the earth's rotation at this latitude is 730. That is wicked fast, yet I can stand in the stream and hardly feel it on my wading boots. Are you following me Beau?" he asked his only companion. Beau lifted his head when he heard his name but then nuzzled in his blanket under the counter when he realized this was one of those conversations that had nothing to do with him.

"Of course the reason for that is, I am traveling at 730 miles per hour, just by standing there. I wonder if people at the equator where the speed is over a 1,000 miles per hour age slower? Who knows? I sure don't. If you know the answer, you're not telling me." He scratched Beau with his foot as he continued to talk. "And with all the other speeds going on, what with our planetary system flying through the universe at something like 45,000 miles per hour and the universe is flying at over two million miles per hour. Yet here we sit, oblivious to it all, thinking we never go nowhere. And that is because everything is relative."

"You know what I think Beau?" Jacob asked as he watched another car from California or Ohio pull up to the pumps outside. "I think some guy just invented time to make himself feel big and in control. We have no control of those things, and dividing the second into parts might help technology calibrate, but it's all a house of cards because there is no second. Dividing something by zero is always zero. God used the idea of days to define the creative periods of his work. Some get so wrapped around their flagpole that it was literally a day, like twenty-four hours. What is that to a God that is not shackled by man's invention of time? Others say each day was a 1,000 years. Just like dividing the second into minuscule fempto seconds," Jacob said looking at Beau who was back asleep, "that's like a trillionth of a second I think. Maybe a quadrillionth, I don't know." Jacob smiled at Beau who must intuitively understand the worthlessness of these words to his life. "Just like the fempto second, the actual amount of time the six days represents that it took God to make the earth only God knows. And if we asked him he would probably remind us again that he is "not bound by man-made inventions, so why are you spinning your wheels on that. It neither helps nor hinders your way back to me.""

Jacob went back to looking at his book and shut his mouth as two men were about to enter the gas station store. He recognized Officer Cochran as he stepped into the store. Jacob tried to avoid this police officer. He was always looking for some free handout because he was a cop. None of the Highway Patrol or Deputy Sheriffs ever did that.

"Jacob, you run a busy place here," Cochran snarled. Jacob could feel the hair raise on the back of his neck. He didn't look up from his book.

"In all the years I have stopped in here and given you my business," Cochran continued, "you have only given back about twenty words. I am here today with a request you double that output."

Jacob figured Cochran had only stopped at his station maybe five times in the last ten years and other than a little gas, he hadn't purchased anything. "What can I do to help officer?" Jacob asked.

"Good," Cochran said a little startled. "Pax and I are looking for a woman, young, dark hair, maybe five feet four or five inches. Pretty thing. Should have passed through here an hour ago, maybe less."

"Haven't noticed," Jacob said. "Some people have come and gone, but I never look at their faces." He was mostly telling the truth but wondered whether Cochran would believe him.

"Here's her picture," Cochran said tossing a photo Paxton had taken with his phone while she had the shotgun in her hands at McKenzie's place. They had swung by the local Walgreens and had some color photos printed when they picked up some basics for their road trip.

"Yes, I do remember her, from a couple days ago," Jacob said. "I can't say when exactly, but within the last week. The days here sort of all run together."

"But not today?" Paxton jumped in.

"Not today," Jacob said. "At least not that I noticed."

Cochran snapped up the photo and looked out the glass door, seeming to decide what his next step should be. He turned to Paxton and said, "Even if she did pass by here, we'd get nothing out of this dimwit. Let's hit the road."

"Bout time," Paxton muttered. "I've got a score to settle."

Jacob said nothing. Cochran's insult didn't upset him. He knew the act he put on around people was mostly to blame. It was only the most ill-mannered that stooped so low as to treat him like an object instead of a human being. Cochran fit into that category, but still, Jacob couldn't be mad at him. He watched them both stomp to their car and pull out like they were teenagers trying to impress a girl with their tire smoke. He couldn't imagine any girl actually being impressed with that and he wasn't either. He was, however, concerned for the safety of a lady he had only briefly met and with whom he had only exchanged a few words.

"Any thoughts Beau?" Jacob asked. "We certainly can't go to the police. Hmm, I wonder..." Jacob hesitated for a moment, not sure he should follow through on his idea, and then opened up his database of purchases to the time frame of 5 A.M. to 8

A.M. yesterday, the 14th. There had been seven purchases. Only one of those made both a purchase at the pump and in the store. 94103 was the zip code for those two purchases. He then did a quick Google search for Harte-Hanks, the Geo-Capture service and jotted down their number. He picked up the phone and provided Mina's name and zip code. Within minutes Jacob had Mina's full name, her address in California, her phone number, and her husband's name. Going to Spokeo, it took him a few more minutes to collect her relatives' names in the Bay Area, her employer, her social media profile and a satellite photo of her home, in this case, an apartment building.

"So she is from California," Jacob noted to Beau. "And she works at Twitter." He called her work number, thinking he could leave a voicemail warning her Cochran was looking for her. He could be anonymous, but at least give her a heads up. He was pretty sure she wasn't an ax murderer, and whatever Cochran was after, this was not official police business.

"Twitter Headquarters," the voice said after two rings.

"Oh, umm, hi, is Mina Gamble there?" Jacob asked, know she wasn't.

"Mina no longer works here," the voice said. "Did you need to speak to her, or to her replacement?"

"When did she stop working there?" Jacob explained. "I need to get in touch with her personally. "She never got this many calls when she worked here," the voice said. "This is the third call this morning asking for her. She quit a couple weeks ago. I was assigned her old work number. Is she in some sort of trouble?"

"No, she isn't in trouble," Jacob said, not sounding very convincing. "I am her investments advisor. I thought she wasn't leaving for another month. You can tell we need to talk more often," Jacob said trying to laugh.

"Right," the voice said.

"It seems her cell number isn't working," Jacob added, not even knowing if she had a cellphone but assuming she did.

"One of the other callers mentioned that too," the voice said. "I don't have her cell number. I am kind of new here. I got her cubicle, but that's all I know, except that she should be on her way to Minneapolis. Her husband got a *too good to be true* job there. She followed him like a good subservient wife. I would have told him to go by himself or told him to go someplace else. I mean, this is 2015. Although Trump could be in the White House next year, so I suppose anything goes, right?"

Jacob hung up the phone. "Loud and clear, San Francisco," Jacob said. Next, he dialed the number of a listed relative. Rubina Vartan. He wasn't sure if this was a male or female name but was pretty sure it was Armenian. That fit Mina's exotic look. His call went to voice mail. "Hey, you got Rubi, leave a message," a female voice said in happy tones.

"Mina might be in some sort of trouble. A police officer is looking for her and it didn't appear he was on police business. Watch out for a guy named Cochran and his sidekick Paxton. They are trouble. Wish I could be of more help, but I don't know what to do." He hung up quickly. That last part sounded dumb, but he wasn't sure how to close up the call.

"Okay Beau," Jacob said. "Enough contact with the outside world. What do you say we close up the store and get in a couple hours of fishing before dark? The pumps can run themselves. Let go," Jacob told himself.

That was Jacob's mantra. Let go. It worked with his mostly catch and release fishing. It worked with his gas station. The place didn't consume him because he didn't consume it. And people. He tried to make a quiet difference as best he could without letting the world connect with him. He visited the populated planet when he had to or felt compelled to as in this case, but it was always a short visit, followed by a extended stay on his one-person world, where the fish were always biting. That is where freedom from incapacitating social pressures blew in the atmosphere.

CHAPTER 14
JACOB

TUESDAY
SEPTEMBER 15, 2015, 2:29 P.M.

J ACOB WATCHED THE MAN PICK up some trash on the top of the gas pump. It was a younger guy. He could tell that from his view inside the station store. The person was too far away for Jacob to know if he was a local customer. The man slammed his hand on the pillar that supported the roof over the pumps. Jacob couldn't tell whether he was mad or happy. Then the man left.

A few minutes later that Laramie police officer drove up. 'What was his name? Cochran, wasn't it?' Jacob asked himself. Even from the store Jacob recognized the bald head and worn out suit that the officer always wore. Cochran was looking around like there was some police investigation going on. He looked at the trash on the top of the pump. Placed it back where he found it. Then he drove off. Jacob went back to reading his book, but couldn't concentrate.

Jacob Critchlow considered himself a quiet observer. It was his second favorite pastime. He wasn't nosey and liked to stay to himself but what people did, especially when they were making decisions, fascinated him. He was uncomfortable with people, but he found them interesting just the same. Jacob thought of himself as the proverbial tree in the forest. He loved the forest to be sure, but more than that, he was the tree in the forest that fell, and no one was there to see it or hear it crash. He was living proof that it still made a sound, or so he hoped. He had fallen a lot, and there was no one there to search out the sound, to ask if he was alright; until one day standing in the middle of a trout stream.

Jacob was enjoying another fishing trip. He stood stationary as the river rushed past him. Staring intently into the water looking for signs of elusive trout, he nearly lost his balance. For a brief moment, it felt like the flow was still, and he was moving, like sitting in a stationary car and your peripheral vision catches the car next to you move, and you press harder on the brakes because you feel like the one in motion. He thought of those photos where the person is moving but is captured as if standing still. The background is a blur as if it were in movement. "The focus flips the perspective. The observer becomes the runner. But even the runner should know he is moving, and the trees stand still. The same goes with love," he told no one because he was alone. "Love, and being loved, can feel like it's rushing past in a blur when in reality, it's love that stands resolute and steadfast, and it's me who is doing the running."

Jacob didn't consider himself a religious man, or even spiritually sensitive. He hadn't grown up with any formal structures in his life. He had no experience with family, or love, or stability. But he had been blessed with an uncle he barely knew existed and who had left him the gas station. Along with the deed to the gas station, his uncle's will included a short note explaining the basic operations of the station and a simple statement. "We all have the gift, we just need to learn how to use it, and that takes faith. I have faith you will do just fine with this station and all that comes with it and with you." his uncle had written.

He had initially wondered what the gift was that his uncle had mentioned. As the days and weeks went on, he turned all of his attention to figuring out how to keep the gas station solvent. Until that day on the river. Jacob had set aside his wondering and simply tried to increase his faith, with the hope that *the gift* would follow.

He had faith, on the dark, cold days, that the sun would come up. Faith that he would not disappoint his uncle in keeping the gas station going, even if he had a hard time connecting with the people that passed through his business and his life. Faith that he would find his path and his place. He never hoped beyond that. He had slowly grown beyond the concept that faith was simply believing that what had happened before would happen again, like the winter would come and seemingly last forever, but eventually, spring would follow. He progressed to seeing faith as believing without proof for something you hoped for or needed. He learned quickly that simply hoping for something did not make it so most of the time. Slowly he developed a model of understanding that faith was a confidence that left no room for doubt of things that Jacob knew to be, but he couldn't understand or explain it with only his physical senses.

Nearly falling into the cold river, the sensation hit him like he had vertigo. His first thought was, "Steady, it's not me that is moving." Then the deeper thought flashed in his mind, "Exactly. Faith demands action. Movement." The understanding hit him hard. Hard enough that again he almost fell into the river. "Yes, it is you that's moving. In fact Jacob, you have been running all your life, but away from, not to anything." He didn't question the formulation of the thought, but the point of the statement made him wince. The tip of the sword of wisdom pierced him, but he still had to endure the long blade of understanding that followed that sharp point. He looked around to ensure he was alone, even though he was sure there wasn't another human within miles of him. Then he spoke aloud, talking to the water, the trout, or anything that might listen. "All my life I have run from pain and the fear of pain. I always thought that was the human condition. Like we're wired to run from discomfort and distress. Stick your hand close to an open flame, and your body pulls the arm back before your mind registers the hurt or even has time to think about it. And unlike some, who sprint short distances, I am a long-distance runner. I stay as far away from people as I can. My fear of pain has kept me from people. No, not just people, but the love of people; my love for them and their love for me. The opposite of fear isn't faith. The opposite of fear is love."

"Love is the foundation of faith," Jacob continued. "So love is the gift my uncle was talking about." What love exactly was, he had no concrete idea, but he knew as he waded out of the water, that his ultimate goal was to find out.

Weeks later he ran across a scripture citation that caught his attention. He had tried to look up the subject of love on the Internet, but all he got was trash; pornography links, romance books, and half-baked definitions that didn't seem to fit the feeling he had that day on the river. He dropped the Internet as his go-to source of answers on this subject. The answers might be there, but the world was working hard to keep him from them. Knowing how lacking his social skills were, he was looking for ways to be more sensitive to the people that bought gas and snacks at his gas station. He thought maybe the Bible might help and he came across some words where Paul had written to the Romans. The words held the same feeling he had discerned standing in the river. "Rejoice with those who rejoice; mourn with those who mourn." It became crystal clear to him with those ten words. "I shouldn't be running from pain or the fear of it. I should be running to others' pains and trying to make a difference. The gift is a promise and a stewardship," he told himself.

Returning to his gas station, he started on a new journey, a part of his life he still kept hidden. He didn't know how to share his faith with the random travelers that passed through his gas station. He didn't have a religious doctrine to share, or some consequence to warn about. So he acted on what he knew; what his own experience had taught him. "Faith is the power that works from the inside, out. Love works the same way, but it also works from the outside, in. Someone might feel your faith, but it only has a limited effect on the receiver. Love, however, has a much stronger and more tangible impact on the receiver. Love is a reptile level passion without faith. Faith without love is an unguided missile. The two together create the twisted pair wire that cancels out external interference and at the same time can create its own magnetic field."

He started by cutting the price on food items when people who looked like they were on hard times made purchases at his station. He never mentioned the secret discount, but he hoped it helped them get to the next point in their travels. He still had a hard time smiling and being friendly, but he was improving.

Thinking about the man at the pump, and then Officer Cochran, Jacob had a feeling it was time for another leg of his own journey. He closed his station, made a call to a young man he often used in emergencies to run things when he was ill, or the trout were biting, quickly cleaned up and put on fresh clothes, and hopped in his old pickup he kept in the back of the store. Before leaving the gas station, he had a thought to stop at the pump that seemed to be so popular. He reached for the bag of Cheetos and was surprised to find a note there. He grabbed it and drove to the Interstate looking for the young man that seemed to be in some sort of trouble.

"Like Quantum physics," he told himself out loud as he pulled out of the gas station. "Everything is in motion if we allow ourselves to see it. Sometimes we can be in two places at once, nowhere at all, or in a place different than the place it was before. Only with observation does it become substance in a single stable place. A belonging place. And only then does time become a substance too. I've found refuge in this cave of a gas station store, but the cost has been to be without substance and without time. I am growing older, but all the clocks have stopped. " He could literally feel time start ticking again as he pulled up to the young man on the highway.

In the early days when he had just taken over the gas station, Jacob felt like he had no substance at all. That's when time became unmoved and immovable. It was as if the world was telling him he was completely dependent on circumstance; entirely dependent on some stranger that walked through his door. He had realized that was his own construction. It was he who was seeing people as objects and that completely voided his own humanity. They were just people with their own imperfections, interests, and passions. As he asked the man if he wanted a lift, he thought, "When we can't change our situation, we must consider changing ourselves. If that potential change is not for the long-term good, we must at least improve our attitude.'

CHAPTER 15
JACK

BEING IN MORE THAN ONE place at a time is a mother-of-small-children's dream. It was Jack's nightmare. A Cochran was chasing Mina, and a Cochran was chasing Jack. Was it the same guy, just passing between realities like Jack changed his shirt, or was it really two iterations of the same person? So why wasn't there another Jack or another Mina? Was the Mina Jack knew already a Mina from another universe? Was there another Jack wandering around in yet a third universe who had never even met Mina? Was the only Mina with another Jack, leaving him out in the cold and no key to open the door? Maybe he was a soccer star in that universe. That though didn't soothe his frustrations, even though Jack had been injured in this universe in his sophomore year of college, ruining any chances of a professional career. The whole idea of quantum superposition was enough to send him over the edge. He tried to understand it with the hopes of finding a way back to Mina, or Mina finding a way back to him.

Jack and Mina had successfully passed a note back and forth to each other, but they were no closer to solving their separation.

It had been nearly three weeks since Mina had disappeared, or was it he who had somehow abandoned her? Something happened on Mina's end, and she had not shown up for the next scheduled "close encounter," as he thought of them. What was it the pastor said when he married them? "Cleave unto one another and be one?" If that was a commandment or something, then either the universes were committing a grave sin, or there was a way to be reunited. McKenzie's story certainly didn't raise his hopes. Was there a limit to the number of note passing sessions the laws of nature allowed?

Wishing he could be in more than one place at a time, in the same universe, Jack had called his new job in Minneapolis and told them a family emergency had come up that would preclude him from taking the job. They were kind and wished him well, but he could tell they were upset. They were counting on him as much as he was excited to take the job, but Mina far outweighed any job. He pushed concerns of how long he could stay unemployed back into a dark corner of his mind. He was living at his parents' home, so at least his costs were low. He still worried about the police finding him. If he were looking for someone, the first place he would look for someone would be a parents' home. He had not contacted Mina's family yet, however. Jack had explained, as best he could, what was going on. His mother had believed him, even though he still had a hard time believing any of this himself.

"Tell me again how you got a call from the Laramie Police again," Jack asked his mother after his explanation of the last few days.

"Well, I was doing the dishes," she began. "It was your father's turn, but his back was bothering him again, so I told him I would do them. You know, I have been noticing that his back especially acts up on his night to do the dishes. I'm glad we had this little talk. I am going to bring that up with him tonight."

"Mom, I need you to get back to the call from the Laramie Police," Jack reminded her.

"Oh, yes of course," his mother said, not at all repentant. "I was thinking about you and Mina and wondering what I could do to help you with your transition, yet so far away. That's what mothers do Jack. And I got this phone call. The man on the other end introduced himself and explained to me about your abandon car. Then I called you."

"Either Officer Cochran was right, and somebody stole the car to play a joke on Cochran, or you got a call from another universe. I can't wait to see that phone bill. Interesting that the car has never shown up. It's probably in another universe and really needs an oil change. My research on multiple universe theories theoretically explains how Mina and I are separated, but I don't remember anything about communications between two realities."

"You and Mina have exchanged notes though, right?" his mother asked.

"Well, yes, sure, but" Jack began to protest.

"You either have, or you haven't," his mother interrupted.

"Okay, mom, we have. But why can't I call Mina?"

"Sun spots, maybe," his mother offered.

"And if it did happen, does that mean there is another Cochran out there? Jack asked.

"You and Mina are in different places, we know that for certain," his mother said. "If there can be two realities, why not three? And if there can be many same realities, why not multiple same people?" his mother asked. "The worlds would have to be populated with somebody."

"How is it you just accept all this?" Jack asked. "This is crazy. The only thing I really know is, Mina is gone."

"Is she gone?" his mother asked him. "Do you still love her?"

"Yes," Jack said, exasperated. "Yes, I love her."

"And what did Mina say in her second note?" his mother asked.

"That love is the power that will bring us back together," Jack said. "But she is still gone."

"*Gone* is such a brutal word, especially the way you say it," his mother said. "When Mina went on that hiking and rafting trip with her cousin, what was her name?"

"Rubi," Jack said.

"That's right, Rubi," his mother said with a smile in her voice. "What a sweet girl. When they went on that trip to Jackson, Wyoming, did you say Mina was gone, or just away for a time?"

"I probably said she was gone, but I know what you mean mother," Jack said. "She was gone in a very temporary way."

Don't be so self-centered then, son," his mother said. "You say it like this is only about you, that she isn't here with you, and that somehow this is her fault. Mina isn't gone; she's just not here right now. Even if someone dies, they aren't gone, at least not the way you say it. If you still love that person, they are never gone. Just like my love for you. And just because we can't see someone, or find peace ourselves because that person isn't by our side physically, doesn't give us permission to curse life and die."

"I'm not cursing or on my death bed," Jack said.

"You don't have to say the words to curse," his mother said. "And the way you are living looks a lot like dying to me."

"So what should I be doing?" Jack asked.

"Live and love, son," his mother said. "Go do something for someone. Get less interested in yourself, and develop a deeper love, not just for Mina, but for everyone. What was the name of that nice police officer from Wyoming? The bald one."

"Cochran," Jack said. "I don't remember describing him as nice, however."

"I think he has found you," his mother said.

"What?" Jack asked. "How do you know that?"

"I have seen this car with Wyoming plates drive by three times this morning," his mother said. The person driving is bald. It's parked three houses down the street."

"When were you going to tell that?" Jack ask

"Do you smell that?" his mother asked. "The berry pie must be done. I need to get it out of the oven." She got up and was gone a few minutes while Jack peeked out the window. She returned and added, "You know that is a miracle."

"What's a miracle?" Jack asked. "That the crazy cop hasn't broken down our door yet?"

"That we can smell and even tell the difference between a fresh berry and when a berry pie has baked just the right amount of time," she answered.

"It is amazing," Jack said, "and I know you are trying to get my mind off of Mina. Thanks."

"There you go again, thinking about yourself," his mother said. "You say Mina, but you mean you—getting Mina off your mind." His mother walked over to the couch by the window where Jack was sitting. "Stop looking out the window and look at me."

Jack turned back to his mother, wishing he had eyes in the back of his head to watch for Cochran.

"I'm your mom, and I am pushing fifty, but I'm not dead yet, and in my day I was no dummy."

Jack smiled, knowing his mom had recently turned fifty-two. "I know mom. You are an intelligent woman with a lot of wisdom. And I love you."

"There are all kinds of molecules floating around in this room," his mother began. "Some are freshly baked pie molecules. Those molecules enter our nose and interact with a sensor receptor. That sensor sends an impulse to the brain that says fresh berry pie and the brain says, yikes, it smells like it is done. Go get it out of the oven. There are some theories of olfaction, but no one is exactly sure how this incredibly complex process works. We can tell the difference between fresh berries, a perfectly baked berry pie, and a burnt berry pie. The molecules are almost exactly the same, but we know the difference. That difference even informs the flavor of the berry. It's a miracle we take for granted."

"If I get a piece of that pie, I promise to try to understand what you are getting at," Jack said with a smile. His mom had told him stories like this since he was a boy. It was part of the reason he went into science, albeit data analytics. His mother's mixture of science, mystery, magic, and religion made it all feel like the greatest adventure there ever was.

"When that berry molecule binds to a receptor in our nose, a process called quantum tunneling is set in motion. You didn't think your old mom knew anything about quantum science did you?"

"No, but I'm not surprised," Jack said. "Go on. You have me hooked."

"Before I go on," his mother said, "did you also know that two very different molecules can also smell about the same?"

"Sure," Jack said. "How many fake products are on the market that taste or smell like something, but absolutely none of the natural essence exists in the product?"

"So how can that happen?" his mother asked. Not waiting for an answer, she continued. "That's where the tunneling comes in. The physical electrons pass through or maybe better said, they jump from the receiving side of the receptor to electric delivery side of the receptor without passing through the space in between. The word scientists use to explain this is a tunnel. This tunneling only works if the bond between the molecule and the receptor vibrates with an exact energy the receptor recognizes. Different molecules can produce the same vibrating bond and thus smell the same, like Sulphur and rotten eggs. And this tunneling happens instantaneously. One theory for this speed is quantum superposition. The bonding molecule is all possibilities at once until it is measured at the other end which limits it to a single possibility. When that happens, time ceases to exist."

"That is quite a theory," Jack said. "And you are telling me this because?"

"Because I want to impress you with my reading and pondering," his mother said, patting his knee. "Jack, really? You don't see the connections?"

"I see it mother," Jack said. "So are you suggesting that quantum tunneling will get Mina and me back together?"

I think that might have happened with the call I got from your police friend outside," his mother said. "And if it can happen for a phone call, it could happen with two people. You just need to find the same energy."

"I can be rotten eggs pretty easily," Jack said, "but I don't know if Mina can be Sulphur."

"No two people smell the same. No, what I am talking about is your kinetic energy. Mina said it better when she described the power of love as a force of nature. Right now you both have powerful potential energy, but not enough active energy to create a tunnel that will connect you two again."

Jack was about to ask how she thought he could convert potential energy into kinetic energy when there was a loud pounding on the door. He jumped on the couch and leaned to the window to look outside. It was Cochran. He looked tired and mean.

"Mom, get upstairs, now. Lock yourself in your bedroom. Call dad and see if he can come home." Jack was looking for some kind of weapon. "And no police." He grabbed a flower vase with flowers in it. He waited for his mother to get up the stairs and he opened the door.

"Are those for me?" Cochran asked. "You shouldn't have." He pushed his way into the living room, looking around like a wild animal. Jack wasn't sure if he was looking for threats or for prey.

"I didn't think you would be so bold," Jack said. "You are pretty far out of your jurisdiction."

"I didn't think you would be such an annoyingly boring target," Cochran spit out. "I only have a few weeks of vacation, and at this rate, your inaction will kill me before I have a chance to kill you. So let's get the show on the road. Are you time traveling from this house? Is this your home base? Don't play with me, Jack. I am so out of patience."

Jack maintained his grip on the flower vase, even though it was no match for the pistol he saw tucked under Cochran's unzipped windbreaker. "I don't know what you are talking about. I don't time travel. You're nuts to think that's real. I am here to look for my wife."

"I'm impressed you made it out of the forest Jack," Cochran hissed. "let alone making it to California." He hesitated to tell Jack he had read the note from Jack's wife that even mentioned the words time travel, but his patience was running thin. He had to get to the bottom of this, now. "I know you are time traveling. I read the notes you two passed to each other at the gas pump. I don't know how you did it, but I was watching, and there is no way it was some trick. You might think I won't kill you to get the information I want. Well, you are right, but I might kill someone close to you. I might make life not worth living and that my friend is a threat I am prepared to follow-through on right now. I know this is your parents' home. I know where your wife's parents live. Unlike you, I have been very busy since arriving here."

"Officer Cochran," Jack said, "if I knew how to time travel I would happily tell you. My wife is stuck in another place, and we still can't figure out how it happened or how to fix things. I don't have anything else to offer you."

"You are not hearing me, Jack," Cochran said, losing his last bit of patience and reaching for his gun. "I know the game you are playing and I,"

Cochran was interrupted by the front door opening quickly and hitting him from behind. It didn't hurt him, but it distracted him and temporarily put him off balance. Jack watched himself swing the flower vase against Cochran's head. The jar shattered and blood from the chards of glass mixed with the water from the vase splattered the door.

As Cochran crumbled to the floor, Jack thanked his dad for his great timing and asked him to run upstairs and get his mom. They were back downstairs before Jack had finished duct taping Cochran's hands together behind his back.

"Mom, thanks for keeping the kitchen junk drawer well-stocked," Jack said, smiling at his mom to hopefully lower her stress level. "Dad, could you help me get this guy into the back of your car, through the house door to the garage? Mom, would it be possible for me to borrow your car?" Without waiting for answers, Jack continued, "He's going to wake up soon. Let's get him into the car and out of hearing range, and I will tell you my plan, and you can give me your thoughts."

Jack's father pulled his car that he had parked several houses down the street, into the garage. Jack and his father carried Cochran into the garage and deposited him in the back seat, also duct taping his mouth and then his feet together. They also put him in a seatbelt that hopefully, he couldn't shimmy out of if he woke up. Within eyesight of Cochran, but with the car doors shut, Jack gathered his parents to him.

"So here is what I think I should do," Jack began. "Dad and I will take Officer Cochran to the Berkeley Botanical Gardens and drop him off. When we return, you and dad go somewhere for a week that Cochran won't know about. Could you do that? I mean, not go to work for a week, dad? I'm afraid he could find you at work and then follow you to where ever you two are at. He did threaten to kill someone close to me."

"We have our timeshare at Tahoe," his father said. "I know it's vacant. I could do most of my work from there for three or four days I guess. Honey, how about you?"

"Lake Tahoe for a week? Count me in" she said. "But what about you, Jack?"

"I'm going to go to Rubi's house in Fresno; you know, Mina's cousin?" Jack said. "Our next scheduled meeting point is supposed to be at St Gregory's, the Armenian Church in Presidio Heights. That's where Mina attended Armenian School after school until she went to college. That's not a hard place for Cochran to find. But, the place after that, our fifth meeting, simply said on her note, "our favorite park bench." Cochran will never know where that is at."

"Where is it?" his father asked. "Or maybe you shouldn't tell me if we get captured and tortured."

"A little melodramatic, dad," Jack said. "If I thought you were in any danger after disappearing, I would keep us together. Our favorite park bench isn't a bench at all. The Park is Yosemite and the bench is a rock at Glacier Point overlooking the Yosemite Valley. It's where I proposed to Mina."

"That will work then," his mother said. "Fresno is only an hour from the Park, right?"

"About that," Jack confirmed. Hopefully, Glacier Point is still open. I expect it is. It's only early October. I hate to miss a meeting, but better to be safe. Best for me to be completely out of the Bay Area anyway. I have got to figure out what the next step to bring us together might be. I don't have any progress to put in a note to her at this point anyway. She knows I love her, so I don't need to send her a note that just says that."

"Jack, she needs to hear that from you more now than ever," his mother chided. "And like our talk earlier somewhere in that love is the answer to your terrible situation. I like your plan but keep in touch. Now that we know what is going on, we will want to know you are safe."

"I will call the timeshare switchboard and connect with your apartment," Jack said, glad his mother mentioned the cell phones. "I don't know if Cochran can track your phones, but it might be best to leave them here at home. I am sure now that he has not brought in any other police. This is for sure a freelance job. I have no idea why he is so hooked on the time travel idea. I wish it were real. I would go back to that gas station and never let Mina out of my sight, even if I had to go into that gross gas station with her." Jack froze, staring off into space.

"Are you okay son?" his mother asked him.

"Yes," Jack said slowly. "I think I just remembered something. The gas station operator."

"Something we need to know?" his father asked.

"No, probably nothing," Jack said. "Well, let's get our friendly neighborhood police officer to the Garden so he can enjoy the flowers.

The drop-off was uneventful. By the time they got to the Gardens Cochran was fully conscious and watched outside, obviously trying to memorize landmarks. They took the tape off of Cochran's mouth and feet. His hands were still behind his back, but Jack knew Cochran could get his arms to the front as soon as he had a minute to sit down. Jack had left Cochran's gun in a dumpster and tossed his wallet in the back of his truck, right after leaving his parents' house and before Cochran was fully conscious. Jack was sure they could drive home faster than Cochran could follow. They would be long gone before he could find his way back to the house. Cochran was uncharacteristically quite as they left him and drove off.

CHAPTER 16
MINA

MINA SAT ON HER FAVORITE rock at Glacier Point, overlooking the Yosemite Valley. She knew right where to sit. This exact spot was where she had perched to see the valley floor just eighteen months ago when they got engaged. She thought she had been the one to coax Jack into coming to Yosemite. She later found out Jack had organized the trip secretly with the help of Mina's favorite cousin. Mina had visited here many times with her cousin Rubina who lived just down the hill in Fresno. Today Mina was forty-eight hours early for her last scheduled connection with Jack but took the drive up here to ensure that crazy Cochran and his henchman Paxton wouldn't know where she was. She was afraid of Cochran. She was terrified of Paxton. They were both nuts.

Just being close to this place gave her a sense of peace. Staying at Tenaya Lodge was convenient to this place, but it brought back memories of their brief honeymoon, spent here and in Carmel on the Monterey Peninsula. They were normally happy memories, but now they made her feel lonely rather than connected with Jack as she had hoped. She had missed their third meeting because of Cochran. Jack had missed their fourth meeting. If this meeting didn't go off right, if they couldn't set up plans for new meetings, they would not know what the next step would be and would be in guessing mode. Perhaps they could start their schedule all over again with both place and time already set, but what date? Cochran was wise to their locations. In reality, if they missed today, that might be it for the rest of their lives. "It had happened before," Mina whispered to herself, thinking of McKenzie and her husband.

'If love really was the answer, how would that happen?' Mina asked herself. Setting up new meetings kept hope alive, but no closer to any real answers. "Maybe Jack has some answers," Mina said out loud. "Jack will have some answers, and he will be at this meeting. Only two days to go. So what I am going to accomplish before we meet?"

Mina stood up, and as she caught a glimpse of the valley floor, she had the sudden thought to reach out to her cousin Rubi. Two days with nothing to do but wait was more than she could face. Mina hadn't even contacted her mother for fear that it would put her family in danger of Cochran and Paxton doing something to get to her. But she was safe here. With excitement, Mina hiked back to her rental car and drove out of the Glacier Point parking lot. A half an hour later she was dialing Rubi's number.

"Hey, you got Ruby, leave a message," the voice on the other end of the call said. It warmed Mina's heart to hear that sing-song voice.

"Rubi, this is Mina. Give me a call at this number, I need to talk to you." Mina read off the number of the Tenaya Lodge and gave her the extension to her room. She turned on the T.V. and waited. Only twenty-two minutes later, the phone rang.

"Hello," Mina said, hoping it was Rubi, but wanting to be cautious just the same.

"Mina, it's Rubi. Where in the world are you and what's going on girl?"

"Are you alone?" Mina asked, still allowing caution to control her own enthusiasm."

"Yes, I'm alone," Rubi said. "You sound, different. Spooked. What did you do? Where are you?"

"I'm okay," Mina lied. "Why are you so worried? I have only been gone a few weeks."

"You are supposed to be in Minnesota, Mina," Rubi said. "This number is in California. In fact, it's my area code. You've got some explaining to do. I got a call, warning me you were in some sort of trouble."

"What?" Mina asked standing up and almost pulling the room phone off the side table. "You got a call? From who?"

"I don't know, but he sounded cute," Rubi said.

Despite her fear Mina smiled. "He sounded cute?" Mina said. "Did you talk with this person long?"

"I didn't talk with him at all," Rubi said. "He left a voicemail. I decided to talk with you before I called him back. Your phone is disconnected. I figured you had already got a new number in Minnesota. So I called your mom. She hadn't heard from you. You have her worried Mina. Now answer me, where are you?"

"Tenaya Lodge," Mina said. "I can't explain over the phone. Can I meet you somewhere, if you aren't busy? I am an hour from anywhere in Fresno, just tell me where."

"Just sit tight girl," Rubi said. "It's still ninety degrees in the valley. I'm coming to you, for some well-deserved fresh, clean, cool air. I will be there in about two hours. How long am I packing for?"

"Ha, you freeloader," Mina laughed for the first time since, since the gas station in Wyoming. "My schedule is a little up in the air, but I will for sure be here for two more days."

"Perfect," Rubi said. "I'll make this a long weekend. Monday, Tuesday, you know what, I'll take Wednesday off for good measure. See you for a late lunch, your treat."

True to her word, Rubi knocked on Mina's door two hours later. Mina opened the door and pulled Rubi in and shut the door. "For sure no one followed you, right?" Mina asked.

"I didn't know I was supposed to be watching," Rubi said. "You said everything was okay. What is going on Mina?" Rubi sat down on the bed, and her eyes bore into Mina. Rubi was built a lot like Mina, just short of five and a half feet tall, dark hair, dark eyes, thin, and full of energy. Jack always said they could be sisters.

"Time for an explanation," Mina said. She had been trying to organize her thoughts since Rubi said she was on her way here. Mina began by explaining their stop at the gas station in Wyoming and ended with her decision to call Rubi. "So what do you think? Am I going crazy?"

"I could have invented a better story if I had dumped my husband," Rubi said. "Your story tops anything I could have dreamed up. So I believe you. I don't get it, but I believe you."

"I don't get it either," Mina said. "It's like my life has stopped, but I am still breathing, still walking, but I am not getting anywhere."

"You just described my life," Rubi said before thinking. "Oh, sorry, that sounded terrible Mina. My head is still trying to get around this whole thing. I just can't think of Jack in another place that you can't get to. So can God get to him, or is there an alternate universe God too? I mean, can God do anything about this?"

"I didn't know you were so religious Rubi," Mina said. "All those years of Armenian school at the church has rubbed off on you."

"I've always believed in God Mina, you know that," Rubi said. "I don't always talk about it, but that's a part of me. If God can know the beginning from the end, then he is not bound by time, right? And so maybe time isn't real. It's just an invention that helps us, but in this case is your worst enemy. We say *infinity* because we don't know how to measure it. We say *chaos* because we don't know how to explain it. We say *future* because we don't know how to control it. And you say *alternate universe* because you don't know how to cross the chasm. It might just be one universe Mina, but with doors we don't know how to open yet."

"Thanks for the hope Rubi," but I'm no closer to opening those doors of a single universe than I was crossing from one universe to the other." Mina turned and looked out the window at the trees, afraid she was going to start crying. If she started crying she knew she would break down completely and that for sure was not going to get her closer to solving this insane situation. She turned back to Rubi better composed.

"Someday I want to introduce you to a Wyoming goat rancher. You would like her. So, tell me about the call you got," Mina said.

"The lady you told me about, McKenzie? Cool. Here, you can listen to it yourself," Rubi said, pulling her phone from her purse. She clicked through to her voicemail and put it on speaker.

"Mina might be in some sort of trouble. A police officer is looking for her, and it didn't appear he was on police business. Watch out for a guy named Cochran and his sidekick Paxton. They are trouble. Wish I could be of more help, but I don't know what to do."

"Well, that wasn't Cochran or his sidekick Paxton," Mina said out loud to herself. "It could be someone else Cochran put up to call you. The voice sounds vaguely familiar though. What's the number?"

"Here it is," Rubi offered. "I looked up the area code. It's a Wyoming number."

"I'm not sure I want to call the number back," Mina said. "I don't know how that works, but I am afraid someone could track the number."

"How about we call Uncle Vinny in Texas and have him make the call," Rubi said. "If anyone decided to bother Vinny, it will be their worst nightmare. It pays to have a black sheep in the family sometimes."

"Oh, my gosh, what a great idea Rubi," Mina said. Vinny was a distant relative that none of Mina's parent's generation wanted to claim but was the favorite of Mina, Ruby, and their cousins. They made the call to Vinny and explained that they got this call and just wanted to ensure it was legit and not some weirdo trying to stalk Mina. Vinny called back less than five minutes later.

"I can't promise you it's legit, but the guy's name is Jacob, and he wasn't there, but his employee was, and he vouched for his boss. You let me know if there is anything I can do for yous two."

"Jacob?" Mina asked herself. "The gas station guy? Maybe the attendant was the employee and Jacob was someone else. So how would they know who I am or that I would be in danger?"

"One way to find out," Rubi said. "Let's give the number a call."

"Let's put it on speaker so we can both listen," Mina said. "You do the talking at first. I still don't want anyone to know where I am."

Rubi dialed the number and set her phone on the side table by the bed. The number rang.

"Hullo," the voice said. It was definitely not the same person as the voicemail. "Not cute," Rubi mouthed to Mina.

"Hi," Rubi said. "I would like to speak with Jacob."

"He's not here," the voice said.

"And where is here? Is this the gas station number?"

"Yup," the voice confirmed.

"When will Jacob be back?" Rubi asked.

"How do I know?" the voice replied, exasperation lacing the reply. "He gets back from who knows where, never explains anything, and then he's off again. Home less than a day. I didn't sign up for this."

"Can I have his cell number?" Rubi asked. "I've misplaced it."

"Sure," the voice said and gave it to her. "And when you talk with him tell him I deserve a raise. I am practically running this place and,"

"And I know," Rubi said, "you didn't sign up for this. I will let him know."

She hung up, and before Mina could say anything, Rubi dialed Jacob's cell number.

"Hello, Jacob's phone," a woman's voice said.

"Hi," Rubi said. "Um, could I talk to Jacob?"

"And who might this be? Jacob's driving." the woman said.

"Um, I'm a friend of Jacob's," Rubi said, looking at Mina whose eyebrows were scrunched up, and shrugged her shoulders.

"Right, Jacob doesn't have any friends, especially of the female persuasion. Did that shedding reptile Cochran put you up to this? I'm hanging up now unless you can offer a better answer."

"Wait," Mina almost yelled. "Is that you McKenzie?"

"Now who on the frozen tundra is that? I have about as many friends as Jacob."

"This is Mina, McKenzie. I am here with my cousin Rubina, Rubi. We need to talk."

"You bet we do Missy," McKenzie said. "Where are you at? And are you alright? Cochran is out after you, and I don't think he would follow-through on his worst threats, but I wouldn't put it past the guy whose leg you nearly shot off."

"You shot at a man?" Rubi asked. "I thought you told me everything."

"Everything important," Mina said to Rubi. "Listen, McKenzie, I wasn't able to be at our third meeting because of Cochran and Jack didn't show for our fourth meeting. Our next and last scheduled meeting is in less than two days. As far as I know, Cochran has no idea where I am at and he has no way of understanding where this meeting will be held."

Tell us where to go, and we will drive on through the night," McKenzie said. "We can be just about anywhere in the Bay area by tomorrow morning."

Mina told McKenzie where they were at, surprising McKenzie, but she got a promise that she and Jacob would arrive late morning tomorrow. McKenzie hung up.

"You shot a man?" Rubi asked. "And that's not an important detail?"

"It was no big deal," Mina said. "Well, it was a big deal because I thought he was going to kill McKenzie."

"He?" Rubi asked. "Not Jacob then. I am getting all these people mixed up. Who's the good guys and who's the bad guys, and you promise you aren't the ringleader of the bad guys?"

"I'm no ringleader," Mina said. "The bad guys are Cochran, the bald cop, and his drinking buddy Paxton. I don't know much about Paxton except that at this point he would love to stomp me into the ground."

"And the good guys?" Rubi asked.

"Well, you of course, and McKenzie," Mina said smiling.

"And Jacob?" Ruby asked.

"I don't know," Mina admitted. "He is an unknown to me. Almost like the wallpaper in this whole thing. If this is the guy who left the voice mail, I guess he is a good guy. We will soon find out."

"So how about we take a walk and you can fill me in on all the other unimportant things," Rubi said, "including what you know about the cute voice."

The next morning, Mina sat up in her bed like a nightmare was just beginning. She looked over, and Rubi was still sound asleep. Then she heard the knock on the door again and realized where she was. "Who is it?" Mina asked, expecting housekeeping. 'What time was it?' she wondered to herself. She looked at the clock, 6:27.

"It's McKenzie. I left Jacob down in the lobby. I wanted to make sure you were up and running, and he is the shy type anyway."

Mina opened the door, and McKenzie walked in. "Good heavens ladies, the day is half over, and you're still in bed. I only got three hours of sleep last night, and I am ready to kick some sense into this day."

Mina and Rubi cleaned up, and introductions with McKenzie were made.

"How about we go down for some breakfast?" Mina asked. "On me this time."

"Do they make all the ladies in your family this beautiful?" McKenzie asked as they walked toward the elevator.

"No," Rubi said. "Unfortunately for us, we're the ugly ones."

"So what does that make me?" McKenzie asked.

"Wonder Woman," Mina said, giving her a side hug as they continued walking. McKenzie was still dressed in her work clothes from the ranch, but she was the solid oak tree Mina needed right now.

They arrived at the Sierra Restaurant off the lobby, and McKenzie walked over to a man who had his back turned to them. McKenzie put her hand on his shoulder, and he turned.

"So this is the mystery voice on my phone?" Rubi asked.

"Yes, mam," Jacob said softly, trying to smile at her and failing. "Sorry for the dire warnings and no follow-up. I wasn't sure who to call."

"I was going to say something cheesy like I love to get calls from tall, dark and handsome voices, but I will just say thanks. It got Mina, and I connected, and I am grateful."

Mina was just staring at him, her mouth partially open.

"You are going to catch a fly on your tongue sooner or later Missy," McKenzie said, looking at Mina.

"You're the FBI agent at the library," Mina said.

"FBI agent?" Rubi asked. "I thought you told me everything, including the unimportant parts, Mina." Rubi bumped her with her hip while not taking her eyes off of Jacob.

"I was, um, just making sure you were safe," Jacob said. "I'm not a stalker or anything. You seemed to be in some serious trouble. I wasn't going to bother you but you sort of commandeered me into service. Since then, McKenzie has explained the real situation, and she and I decided to come back to California to make sure you were safe from Cochran and his friend."

"I had such a scrambled mind that day," Mina said. I don't remember even thanking you. Thank you. Now wait, are you the same guy as the baseball-capped gas station attendant?"

Jacob looked down at the floor for a moment and then slowly lifted his eyes to look at Mina. "Yes, that's me. Actually, I own the gas station. And please, please, forgive me for the bathroom. I was chewed out all the way here by McKenzie."

"You were in a bathroom with Jacob?" Rubi asked. "What does he need to apologize for Mina? What more haven't you told me?"

No one acknowledged Rubi's questions. Rubi shrugged her shoulders and asked, "So Jacob, tell me about Wyoming. Do you ever go fishing?"

As Jacob's head jolted up to look directly at Rubi, Mina interjected, "Jacob, don't get her started. The first time we came to Yosemite Rubi took me fly fishing. We were what, only nine or ten years old? Rubi's family lives on the San Joaquin River, and she grew up with a fishing poll in her hand. If you let her, she will talk all day about flies, and rods, and I have no idea." Mina stopped talking and looked at Jacob, then to Rubi. It was like there was this laser beam connecting their eyes.

"I like fishing too," Jacob said. "That's me and Beau's favorite pastime actually."

"Your beau?" Rubi asked with a sudden sadness in her eyes.

CHAPTER 17
MCKENZIE

COCHRAN AND PAXTON WERE GONE, but McKenzie still lay crumpled on her front porch. She didn't move until she heard her goats whining so loud she thought they would bust a gut. It was getting cold. She wasn't sure how long she had been out but was pretty sure she had been slipping in and out of consciousness for some time. McKenzie tried to sit up, but couldn't move. For the first time today she was scared. Starting small and simple, she wiggled her toes and her fingers. They seemed to be working, but maybe their movement was her imagination. Concentrating on her right arm, she attempted to reposition it. Her arm moved, and it wasn't her imagination. It took her at least half an hour, but she got herself to a standing position. By nightfall, she had completed her chores and was sitting at her kitchen table eating some homemade goat cheese and crackers for dinner.

The memories of Mina and the confrontation with Cochran were coming back with a vengeance. "At least Mina wasn't here when those goons came a lookin," McKenzie told herself. Without bothering to do the dishes, one the chores she always did every night, she made the arduous climb up the stairs and slept without moving until it was time for morning chores. The next day melted into the next and soon a week was gone and she hadn't heard from Mina. McKenzie was feeling like herself again, ready to take on the world. Near the end of the second week of chores and loneliness, she called a neighbor who was only twenty miles away, to see if their teenage son could watch the place and handle the chores for a week or so while she visited a friend. She had hired this teen in the past when she had a hernia surgery and once when she drove to Cheyenne to purchase a new truck.

She wasn't sure where or how she would find Mina, but knew her last name and the town her parents lived in. Having graduated from Stanford, albeit what amounted to one hundred years ago in Silicon Valley time, she felt pretty certain she could pick up Mina's trail.

The day she had scheduled to leave she stopped for gas at Jacobs. Thinking to pick up a few snacks and some bottled water for the road, she stepped inside the station. Jacob had a pimply towheaded young man behind the counter. Jacob was probably off fishing again, she thought. He certainly wasn't cleaning the bathroom. As she turned to leave the store, she literally bumped into Jacob as he opened the door.

"McKenzie," Jacob said.

"Jacob," McKenzie replied. That was usually the full extent of their conversations. Today, however Jacob appeared to try to smile and looked directly at McKenzie. He had strikingly handsome eyes she realized.

"I didn't take you for a junk food junkie," Jacob said.

"I'm going on a little road trip. Going to look for that young filly whose husband disappeared from here a few weeks ago. My theory is all the life was sucked out of him when he entered your bathroom."

"Yeh, I got to do something about that," Jacob said, looking at the floor again. He stood in the doorway, not allowing McKenzie to pass. Something was on his mind, and he was trying to put it into words.

"Time for me to go, Jacob," McKenzie said, trying to get by him.

"Tell me about it," Jacob said. "Just came from there."

"Fishing in the Sierras?" McKenzie guessed out loud.

"Fishing?" Jacob asked. "In a manner of speaking, but in the San Francisco Bay area. Listen, McKenzie, I might be able to help."

"Help what?" McKenzie asked.

"Help you," Jacob said, "and Mina Gamble."

"What?" McKenzie spat. "Jacob Critchlow, you better start explaining yourself right now. If you are tied up in this, or if you are working for that varmint Cochran, I will take you over my knee right here, right now."

"Relax McKenzie," Jacob said. "Let's step outside and I can tell you what I know." Jacob explained his run in with Cochran, his phone message, and his trip to California and meeting Mina in the library. "One good thing about my practiced talent of being nearly invisible, Cochran didn't recognize me, and neither did Ms. Gamble when I escorted her out of the library."

"And you just got back?" McKenzie asked.

"Yep, about ten minutes ago. Why?" he asked.

"Well," McKenzie paused, "are you ready to get back in the seat and drive all night?"

"Sure," Jacob said. "But you have to explain to what is really going on. All I know is, there is a young lady that is in a hog trough full of trouble. I would prefer to stay anonymous, or at least in the background, though."

"Leave your bathroom out of this," McKenzie said. "I want to leave right now, if you're ready."

"How about we take my truck," Jacob offered. "It gets twice the gas mileage as your monster."

"Talk nice about my truck or it might eat you up and spit you out," McKenzie said. "Okay then, let's go."

It took McKenzie a while to break the silence of their drive to ask some questions. She wasn't afraid, but the folks around her neck of the woods were pretty private and independent. She didn't want to break down those walls, if Jacob wanted them in place. Finally, she asked, "So why are you really doing this Jacob? You know as well as I do that this is not you."

"Well, it is me," Jacob said. "I just stopped running from it. What you seek is seeking you, Rumi said."

"This is going to be some interesting drive," McKenzie replied. "Maybe first I should explain, as best I can what is going on. Hold tight to that steering wheel. This is quite the story." McKenzie told Jacob everything about her husband's disappearance long ago, her research, her time with Mina, and how Cochran fits into this story.

"You know it worked, I think," Jacob said. "Ms. Gamble was pretty emotional when we bumped into each other. We didn't talk much, but she had a note, like you described. She kept it in her pocket, but she wouldn't let go of it, so I saw it a couple of times as we escaped Cochran out a back door of the library. Now I understand why that piece of paper was so important to her. Even then, her grasp on that paper got me thinking about the things I wouldn't let go of. My fear of connecting with people. My fear of loving them."

McKenzie was still too focused on her own concerns to notice Jacob's opening of his deeper emotions and anxieties. "I was afraid it wasn't going to work," McKenzie said. "I thought it might have just been some anomaly that it worked for me a Frank a few times. It didn't work after the first successes. I decided not to add any worries to her plate, so I didn't express those fears. I figured if it didn't work, she could curse me and move on with her life."

They drove in silence for a time and then McKenzie added, "My other fear I almost mentioned to Mina when we decided to leave a note for Jack, was that Frank simply moved on and that might happen to her Jack also. It's very possible Frank met another McKenzie and abandoned the original, or who knows, maybe I'm the copy."

"What is a copy if both are the very same person?" Jacob asked. "If you never found him and your husband was with another McKenzie, what would happen to the very real experiences, to children, friends—would the other pick up those memories and wisdom?"

"I don't know," McKenzie said, sounding far off. "I do know the love doesn't die; it's not split in two, or diluted."

You're talking like there really is another McKenzie," Jacob said. "Something else bothers me about what you explained. You said observation is what defines the reality. There can be two or more realities until it is observed and then the one observed is the new and only reality, right?"

"That's the Schrodinger's Cat theory," McKenzie said. "Quantum Mechanics says they have proven this in small lab experiments. Of course, I'm not sure they know what is really going on before they observe it. Smells like a self-fulfilling prophecy, or maybe I just want it to be."

"My problem with the observation theory is," Jacob continued, "I don't think you can define reality by simply seeing. That's just a picture, not a heartbeat. The picture, the observation snapshot, isn't the whole picture because it isn't alive."

The conversation retreated to each of their minds as the long highway stretched before them.

McKenzie's plan was to find Mina parents and from there contact Mina. If they could, they would distract Cochran so

Mina's meetings could happen without complications. Hopefully, some new meeting places and times could be exchanged and in between those meetings they could get closer to a real solution. Somewhere in eastern Nevada, Jacob's phone rang. Both Jacob and McKenzie were running out of steam and McKenzie took the phone so Jacob could continue to concentrate on his driving.

"Do you know anyone from a 559 area code?" McKenzie asked.

"I don't know anyone from any area code," Jacob said. "Be careful, it might be Cochran, or one of his people."

"He can't shot me over the phone," McKenzie grumbled. She answered it. "Hello, Jacob's phone," McKenzie said.

"Hi," a woman's voice said. "Um, could I talk to Jacob?"

"And who might this be? Jacob's driving." McKenzie replied.

"Um, I'm a friend of Jacob's" the woman said.

"Right, Jacob doesn't have any friends, especially of the female persuasion. Did that shedding reptile Cochran put you up to this? I'm hanging up now, unless you can offer a better answer."

"Wait," another woman's voice said. "Is that you McKenzie?"

Both McKenzie and Jacob recognized Mina's voice. Mina quickly explained where she was and how to get there. Jacob and McKenzie switched off driving through the night and arrived at the Tenaya Lodge the next morning, tired and hungry.

"I'll stay down here in the lobby," Jacob said. "I can watch for Cochran."

"And you won't have to face two ladies who might not be ready to greet the world yet," McKenzie added. "I know you're shy, or maybe that's not it, maybe chronic introvert is a closer diagnosis, but I don't think you have a social anxiety or anything like that. Just remember, you have a lot to offer the world, Jacob."

"Thanks, Doc," Jacob said, smiling. "Don't get your hopes up. I would much rather be on a river with a fly rod and my dog."

"Then, why are you here?" McKenzie asked.

"Someone needs help and maybe I can make a difference," Jacob said without hesitation.

"Uh, huh," McKenzie said. "Don't get your hopes up that you are going to be able to maintain that social pariah status. I'll be back shortly. Then maybe we can get some real food in our gullets."

McKenzie returned with Mina and her cousin twenty minutes later. Jacob wasn't sure what Mina would think, or if she would even recognize him from the San Francisco Library, or his gas station for that matter. He was actually surprised when she did. What he wasn't prepared for was Mina's cousin. He had never imagined there was a girl like this walking around anywhere in the world that looked like her, smelled like her, talked like her, or had interests like her. He really liked her and hadn't yet said a word to her.

They walked into the hotel restaurant, McKenzie leading the way and Jacob reluctantly joining the party at the end of the line. It ended up Rubi sat next to Jacob. He actually preferred this as he only had to contend with her in his peripheral vision. He could more comfortably look straight ahead at McKenzie, the only person in the group he could look at and not have to fight the urge to just look at his plate. McKenzie seemed to understand and gave him an encouraging smile.

"I know it's not fair to anyone in this room, but I think of how much money these people have spent to get a glimpse of Yosemite," Mina said as they waited for the waitress to come to their table. Some people have spent thousands of dollars to get a glimpse of Yosemite Falls. And here we all are, for a totally different reason. I used to be in the high expectation crowd. I wasn't a hedonist, at least I don't think that was me, but I had a lot and expected more. "

"From what you have told me about the science of your predicament, if I understand it right," Rubi said, "it appears gravitational waves are the universe's revenge for the man-made practice of "For those who have, much will be given.""

"I know what you mean," Mina said. "I had it all and it seemed like the rule was, because of that I got to have even more. All I want now is to have my husband back, that's it."

"I used to think that way," McKenzie added. "He who has the gold makes the rules and all that, but that is just sour grapes. God knows our hearts and blessings come to those who need them, and they will for you Mina, no matter what happens tomorrow. But I feel really positive about this. Great things are going to happen tomorrow."

"Humankind tends to give selfishly," Jacob said. "God is not restrained by our shortsightedness or zero-sum perspective. Giving doesn't impoverish him, and being avaricious doesn't increase his wealth. He is discreet at times, almost anonymous, but I agree with McKenzie, the blessings are all around us."

The table went quiet, with everyone looking at Jacob. He was grateful the waitress chose that moment to approach their table. Everyone chose the breakfast buffet and soon each were selecting from the oatmeal, the eggs and bacon, the yogurt and granola, and the fresh fruit. It truly was a feast and each felt just a little more grateful for it. As everyone settled and began eating, it appeared all were starving, Jacob cleared his throat.

"Listen, sorry for the thoughts, Jacob said. I don't get a chance to talk to a lot of people." He looked at McKenzie and her slight frown caused him to blush. "Well, that's not true. I go out of my way not to talk to people, so I might say some odd things now and then. I am just glad to be here to help if I can."

"Thanks, Jacob, McKenzie said. "For the ride, the conversation, and for paying for breakfast."

Jacob laughed as he hadn't even thought about offering to pay. This was his first meal out in over a year and his first ever meal with three ladies. "No problem McKenzie."

The meal continued with small talk, but Jacob stayed quiet. He loved listening to how easily everyone entered and exited the flowing discussion and how turns in topic and mood flowed like his rivers back home. At one moment there was some froth from a hidden rock and then it quickly disappeared an instant later downstream. At one point as the food was mostly disappeared, Jacob reached for the water pitcher at the same time as Rubi, and their hands touched. It didn't seem to bother Rubi, but Jacob pulled his hand away, grabbed his napkin in his lap for something to do. He wiped his mouth and then stood and said he was going to go take care of the bill.

"Jacob's a good boy," McKenzie said when he was out of hearing range. "He's honest, smart, and he handles a steep learning curve like a math genius takes to derivative calculus. He's had a hard life that has been pretty much void of people. He's got a lot to give and he is only here because he cares. You know he was only home from California fifteen minutes when I talked him into returning with me. Let's all give him the distance he needs as he drinks from the social fire hydrant we take for granted."

"I think he's awesome," Rubi said with a light chuckle.

"The country mouse can get pretty awestruck by the city mouse," McKenzie said. "Be gentle with his feelings. Wow, I'm starting to sound like I'm his mother." Abruptly changing the subject, McKenzie added, "After a nap, assuming Jacob and I can get rooms, what's the plan for the day?"

"I made reservations for you already," Mina said. "The rooms should be ready early too—I sort of pushed a little, but I didn't expect you until about ten or eleven. Let's get together again about three. You shouldn't sleep too long, or you won't be able to sleep tonight. We can sort through the next steps then. We have until tomorrow at ten. That's when my connection with Jack is set for. It will only take about thirty minutes to get to Glacier Point from here."

"I will get Jacob then and check in," McKenzie said. "See you gals at three here in the lobby."

As exhausted as he was, Jacob couldn't sleep. An hour later he was in the lobby doing some people watching.

"Couldn't sleep?" Rubi asked as she and Mina walked up to him.

"Just afraid I won't sleep tonight if I nap now," Jacob said standing and not sure what to say next.

"We are going for a short hike," Mina said. "Want to come?"

"Umm, sure," Jacob said. "Let me grab a bottle of water and I'll meet you out front. Do you need anything I can pick up at hotel shop?" The girls said they had everything they needed and he escaped. They turned as if to leave and turned around again to watch Jacob walk off.

They ended up driving up to the Mariposa Grove and took the easy walk around the Giant Sequoias. Jacob felt like he was standing in the middle of a trout stream back in Wyoming, even though there were many tourists and the earth under him was dry. It was peaceful and another amazing gift that almost brought him to tears.

"My dad used to bring me here," Rubi said suddenly standing beside him as they both stared at the Grizzly Giant. "I think this is one of the largest trees in the world. I know there are a few larger ones, but I've never seen them, so this is the biggest to me. And it's over two-thousand years old."

They stood there in silence, then Jacob asked, "If there are alternate universes, can you imagine this tree having a double? It just feels impossible."

"And yet, I have listened to Mina and is it any more crazy to consider the complexity of a human being having a double in another universe?" Rubi asked.

"I am still skeptical," Jacob said. "I believe Mina, I believe McKenzie, but I also believe my own heart. That's the splitting I am struggling with."

"Jacob the Splitter," Rubi said.

"What's that?" Jacob asked in surprise.

"Nothing," Rubi said, surprised at his reaction. "I was mostly just joking. But of all of us, you are the one who seems to see this most clearly. We are all seeing pieces, you are seeing all the pieces. I've not said anything to Mina, but I think once you have put these pieces together you are going to solve this puzzle."

"I had an uncle I barely knew. He's the one who left me the gas station I run in Wyoming. He left something else to me. A note. The last lines say, "We all have the gift, we just need to learn how to use it, and that takes faith. I have faith you will do just fine with this station and all that comes with it and with you." I have believed all these years that when he said *We all* he meant every one of us. Lately, I have been thinking he might have meant, him, me, the family I never knew. Maybe it's my fault that Jack and Mina were split apart."

"I don't see how that could be Jacob," Rubi said. "How can one person so directly affect another, in such an unbelievable way?"

"McKenzie told me on our drive here that she has a theory about all this," Jacob began. "Her answer to why now?"

"And this theory has to do with you being the cause?" Rubi asked.

"Not exactly," Jacob said. "She hasn't gotten that far in her theory yet. She said that the global mass, the sum total of humanity, has been below the threshold of mitosis. Humanity is beautifully diverse, but we are cohesive. Some measure of love beyond ourselves has kept us together. But something happened in the 1970s. Whether that is the size of humanity, its mass, or the ratio of the level of love versus that mass, or simply the diminishing faith and resultant depletion of love in the world, she isn't sure. That is why this splitting phenomenon is a new event. She supposes it could have happened at other volatile points in history, but her Frank was at the wrong place at the right time. Some disruption broke them apart. She believes it was a gravitational wave and soon we will be able to measure that."

"And your theory?" Rubi asked.

"It doesn't matter specifically what ratio of love or cohesion, or mass changed. Not to Frank and Jack anyway. Maybe to humanity at some point because we may be facing even bigger issues than a few disappearances at a remote place in Wyoming," Jacob began. He turned to Rubi and almost lost his nerve, but then asked, "May I hold your hand?"

Rubi said nothing and her eyes never left his, but her hand found his and she gave it a squeeze. "Go on. I want to hear your theory."

Jacob turned back to the giant tree and continued. "So I will leave it to McKenzie and Mina to sort out the science of the quantum mitosis as she calls it, the big split. Of all the places in the world that this has happened, that has ever been reported or put down as an unexplainable missing person was at my gas station. Either me or my uncle were the only people there. When you said Jacob the Splitter, you put words to the thoughts I have been having and the real reason I couldn't get to sleep today."

"Other than you just happened to be there, you are blaming yourself?" Rubi asked.

"It feels more logical, and I think that is what my uncle was talking about in his note."

"Well, if you think so, then give you uncle's note a chance to prove itself. He says you will be able to learn how to use it. That just goes back to what I said earlier. I think you are going to solve this. Come on, let's go find Mina." She squeezed his hand, let go and walked off.

Staring at the masterpiece of nature or God's handiwork Jacob felt small. He also felt exhausted. Not so much from the lack of sleep, but the amount of effort it had taken him to be by this girl, to talk to her about things he had never expressed to anyone, and to hold her hand. He felt like a ten-year-old who had just asked a girl for a kiss for the first time. Completely full and completely drained.

"Jacob the Splitter," he said to the tree. "After this meeting tomorrow, time for me to split, so I don't cause anyone else any irreparable harm."

CHAPTER 18
COCHRAN & COCHRAN

COCHRAN TORE THE DUCT TAPE that bound his hands, with his teeth. He was free before Jack's car was out of the Garden. Cochran ran to the buildings near the parking lot. He knew his wallet was gone, but he had four fifty dollar bills in his shoe. He always carried that cash in case his car broke down outside of Laramie. He almost never thought about it, until the ride to this park, or whatever it's called by the locals. He offered to pay for a phone call but knew the reception desk attendant would allow the call and not break the half-C note.

He had a taxi take him back to his truck. He laughed out loud when he found his wallet and keys to his truck tossed in the back. "Nice neighborhood," he said to himself. "Even in Laramie the wallet would have been long-gone and maybe even the truck. Chumps."

He walked back to Jack's parents' home. He knocked politely, and then went around to the backyard, peering through windows. No obvious alarm system. Quietly breaking a glass pane in the back door, he entered the home and confirmed everyone was gone. Other than drinking some water and wiping to remove any finger prints, he didn't take anything and left quickly, in case a nosey neighbor called one of his brothers in arms. He would have a hard time explaining his breaking and entering.

"The parents are a dead end," Cochran told himself. "They would be if they were my parents." He drove to the first commercial area he found, a Taco Bell parking lot, to get out of the neighborhood and to think.

"The thing about the future is, We've never been there; if we had that would be the present," he heard his training officer tell him decades earlier. "The trick is, when you hit a dead end, think present. What would the person you are looking for be doing, right now? Time zig zags. It's not a one-way street to the future. There are plenty of intersections you can cross where you might find what you are looking for. In fact, there is no future, only a hope or belief in a new present."

Cochran sat there for a few more minutes thinking about his training officer from years ago and then said, "His mom." He remembered that prank call that Jack said was real. He pulled out the police report he had brought with him and found the address of Jack's mom in the emergency contact information. It was the same address that he had just left. Nothing there. Next to Jack's parent's address, however, was Mina's parent's address. He immediately drove to it and watched a nice looking pickup, just a little older than his own, pull away from the curb just a few houses down. "Nice taste, mister," Cochran mumbled. He got out and started walking up to the door.

"You forgot the number already?" a lady said as she walked out the front door.

'This has to be Mina's mother," Cochran thought to himself. Before he could verbalize a thing, she handed him a business card. He looked at it and it had a name and contact information on it.

"I thought of this and hoped to catch you before you drove off," the lady said. "And if you hear from her, young man, you tell her that her mother is waiting for a call." She turned and walked back into the house.

Cochran stood there on the sidewalk, having not said a word, with contact information for a Rubina Vartan. He had no idea what had just happened. Rather than press his luck he walked back to his truck and drove back to the Taco Bell. He asked to see the manager and then asked to borrow the phone, handing him a $50 dollar bill. "I need forty in change, but ten ought to cover a local call."

Cochran called the number and an older man answered. "I am looking for Rubina Vartan. Is this a good number?"

"It would be a good number if she were ever home," the man replied. "You just missed her. She said something about driving up to Tenaya Lodge. A matter of life and death. Everything is a matter of life and death with my Rubi."

"Tenaya Lodge, got it thanks," Cochran said. He asked about Tenaya Lodge to the Taco Bell manager, got directions and left, with three green burritos. He arrived at Tenaya Lodge an hour later. He went to the front desk and asked if a Rubina Vartan had checked in yet. The Front Desk Clerk said a reservation had been made, but that she hadn't checked in yet. He went back to his truck and found a quiet paring spot in the lower lot, leaned back in his seat, closed his eyes and was asleep a minute later.

* * *

Cochran and Paxton parked in front of Mina's mother's home. "You stay here Pax," Cochran said. "I want this to be a friendly visit. Keep a watch on the street. I'll be back in a few minutes." Paxton grumbled something unintelligible and slumped down in the seat. Cochran grabbed a loose-leaf note-book that had a couple plastic holders for the few CDs he liked to listen to.

"Hello, do I have the mother of Mina Gamble?" Cochran asked with his best friendly smile.

"Is something wrong?" the older lady asked. Cochran could see where Mina got her looks. This lady was elegant and Cochran knew she was closer to his age, but looked closer to Mina's age.

"Oh, no mam," Cochran said. "I am from security at her old job and had some forms for her to fill out. HR's fault, but I need to get a hold of her. Is she here? This will only take a minute of her time, promise. Hopefully she hasn't left for her new job yet."

"I'm sorry, she is gone," Mina's mother said. "I haven't heard from her and beginning to get worried. Your visit gave me a start."

"That's too bad," Cochran said, scrunching his eyebrows. "Is there a number I can reach her at that she might have left with you. It seems her cell phone isn't working."

"I know, I have been calling it the past few days too," Mina's mom said. "You're in luck though. Mina's cousin Rubi called last night. It seems Mina lost her phone and turned off the ser-vice. She just had a minute and called Rubi because she had her number memorized. You know how that speed dial thing takes the place of actually remembering important numbers. Mina promised to call in a day or two. Leave me your number and I will call you when I get her new number."

"I don't want you to be bothered with our HR's incompe-tence," Cochran said with new hope. "How can I get a hold of Mina's cousin?"

"I have her number on my phone," Mina's mother said. "Just a moment."

"Is this a case of the pot calling the kettle black?" Cochran said with a broad smile.

"Oh, I see what you mean, young man," she said, laughing.

"Young man?" Cochran said falling out of character for a moment. "I am old enough to be your daughter's father."

"I call every man young man, but in your case it fits," she said. She left the door open and walked into the house. Cochran considered going in, but opted to stay put. He was getting what he was looking for.

She returned and was pushing buttons on her phone. "I know it's in here somewhere. This new phone is really giving me fits."

"Here, let me help," Cochran said reaching out his hand.

She handed him the phone and he quickly thumbed through it. "Rubi's last name?" Cochran asked.

"Vartan," she said. "Rubina Vartan."

Cochran found the name and quickly wrote down the phone number and he also memorized the address. "Thank you, mam. I will be on my way. You have a wonderful day." He quickly walked back to his truck, hopped in and wrote down the address. He handed it to Paxton. "Put this in your phone and get us there quick."

Neither Cochran nor Paxton noticed the similar looking truck pull up just a few houses away. As they drove off they also didn't notice that the other truck shimmered slightly as it dissolved into thin air.

Twenty minutes later they were parked two houses down from Rubina Vartan's address.

"I know you are a cop and used to these stake out things," Paxton said, but I am hungry and it's almost lunch time. Why don't we just go knock on the door and get this ball rolling?"

"Once the ball starts rolling," Cochran said, not looking at Paxton, "it sometimes gets out of control. Let's just wait here for a while. I 'm not much of a good example, but patience is the most important tool of police work."

"Oh get off it, Cochran," Paxton spat. "I want some action. I'll go break down the door if you won't."

Before Paxton could get out of the vehicle, they both saw a young lady leave the house and get into a car. She was in a hurry.

"Bingo," Cochran said. "That wasn't too hard was it?"

"How do we know this is the Rubi girl and that she will lead us to Mina?" Paxton asked as they pulled away from the curb.

"We don't," Cochran said. "But here's our choices. We follow her, and she either leads us to Mina or she doesn't. If Mina is hiding out here, she will be there when this girl returns. If we stop to see if Mina is here, we lose this girl, who might be going to see Mina right now. The goal is to find Mina, not break doors."

They followed this young lady all the way out of Fresno and up Highway 41. Forty minutes into the drive, even Cochran began to have doubts. He didn't want to admit a mistake to Paxton so he kept following. They pulled into the Tenaya Lodge a little over an hour later. They parked. Cochran turned to Paxton. "I know, stay here and watch the parking lot," Paxton said.

Cochran smiled, got out, and entered the lobby. Rubi didn't know who he was and he found a seat by the central fireplace where he could see the entrance, the front desk, the restaurant entrance, and the elevator alcove.

* * *

He woke slowly, trying to sort out where he was. He got out of his truck. It was dark. Walking back into the hotel, the walk helped him feel better. On a hunch he asked if a Jack Gamble had checked in. He had. Cochran smiled and asked when he was checking out, so he could check out on the same day. He got a room, with the plan to check out day after tomorrow. Knowing now that Jack would be here for a while, he walked into the restaurant and treated himself to a steak.

With a full stomach, Cochran stretched out on his bed. This trip had presented its challenges, but he had done some good police work. He had found Jack against all odds. "Still no time travel discoveries, but I know something really screwy is going on here. Maybe tomorrow." The adventure had been rejuvenating. He felt like a police officer for the first time in a long time. That reminded him of why he had become a police officer. He pushed that back into his subconscious. He still wanted it all, to feel in control. His will over his boring, dead-end, meaningless life. He fell asleep and didn't move until the sun came through the window the next morning.

Showered and the only clothes he had with him ironed, so he wouldn't look like a bum and attract attention, he went downstairs for an early breakfast. Knowing Jack's room number he had tried to get a room close to his. The best he could do was in the same alcove, but across the hallway. He had hoped to get a room next door so he could try to listen through the wall. He cracked his door in hopes of hearing him leave. He sat on the other side of the door on the floor in his room, waiting.

Jack finally left his room about 9 A.M., after having room delivery breakfast an hour earlier. Cochran left seconds later and took the stairs, expecting Jack would take the elevator. Leaving the hotel, Jack got in a car and drove slowly out of the parking lot. Cochran was not far behind. They arrived at Glacier Point a half an hour later. Cochran wasn't sure where Jack was going or what he planned to do here, but it wasn't sightseeing. Cochran noticed Jack was particularly interested in one rock out-cropping. He stayed back in a small grove of trees.

* * *

Cochran watched Mina and Rubi leave with some guy. He overheard, without moving from his seat where he had his head buried in a newspaper, that they were going on a hike.

"We should get to Glacier Point early tomorrow, Mina. It's late in the year, but still plenty of tourists. You know Jack will be doing the same. We will want to make sure no one is planning their picnic right where the exchange is supposed to take place."

"Let's get some exercise," Mina said. McKenzie needs her rest. We can talk later tonight and plan to have an early breakfast and head up there by nine."

Cochran wasn't sure who the guy was, and then he remembered—the FBI agent in San Francisco. He had to really be careful, but he had a head start on them. He waited for them to leave the hotel and then went over to the Front Desk and asked for directions to Glacier Point. He drove up to Glacier Point and walked around to check out all the possible ingress routes and eventually found a perch that offered a view of the entire area. He would avoid any possibility of being seen. The FBI was an additional complication. Maybe this was a government project. That he knew about it added to the dangers, but also to the possibilities. He would be at Glacier Point very early the next morning. He and Paxton drove down the hill and stayed at the Comfort Inn in Oakhurst.

Paxton and Cochran arrived first the next morning and were seated by an outcropping of Manzanita enjoying the fresh mountain air—not that much different from home. Cochran was surprised he actually felt a bit of homesickness. They watched a bus of Japanese tourists get off their bus and walk around. Nothing else happened until Paxton, and then Cochran saw Mina, a young lady who must be Rubi, the FBI agent, and McKenzie. It was all Cochran could do to keep Paxton from charging at Mina.

"Just wait," Cochran said. "Patience and perseverance got us this far. You can wait a few more minutes."

* * *

The next to arrive was Jack, followed by Cochran. Jack parked close to the trail that led directly to the viewpoint. He was a half an hour early but wanted to make sure he was in the right place at the right time. He had worked on a note all night long that told of his love for Mina and dates and times for five additional meetings. He expected Mina to also provide a list of meetings, so he spaced his dates out and told Mina in the note that if there were any conflicts, her list would take precedent.

Jack stood on the rock where he had proposed to Mina. His heart ached. He could hardly breathe. How much of their love was really about him? Was his mother right? Did he want her back for him, or did he want her back for her? He realized he wanted her back for them. He sat down cross-legged on the rock. Hoping he looked like someone doing some sort of strange yoga meditation, he stretched out his arms and rested them on his knees. One hand, palm facing up, the other hand facing down. "I feel like a Sufi dancer," he mumbled to himself. "Except the world is spinning and I am still." He held the note in his hand ready to drop it. His watch said two minutes to the time. At thirty seconds he would slow his breathing to barely a sigh.

* * *

Jacob and Rubi took their place near the trail coming from the parking lot, planning to keep any groups from climbing the rock that Mina was now approaching. Jacob turned his attention to the trail. Rubi watched Mina. McKenzie found a viewpoint close the other side of the trail coming from the various view sites of the valley below. Five minutes until the connection. It felt peaceful and still like the earth had stopped rotating. Even the birds and the insects seemed to stop their fluttering and buzzing. All of nature was holding its breath.

It happened before Cochran could stop him. Paxton got up and charged Mina. Cochran, trying to break out of his own reverie could only get out one word, "Wait."

In the silence of the moment, that one word broke the glassy stillness and chards of time fell on the rock making a racket that startled every being nearby. As birds took flight, Jacob turned around to see what was happening. He saw a man charging Mina. Then he saw Jack appear, sitting right in front of Mina. Mina saw him too, and she screamed, whether for the sight of Jack or Jack getting up to protect her from a crazed Paxton, no one knew. Cochran was running forward in an attempt to stop Paxton. Jack dodged Paxton who was a raging bull and unable to turn to catch the now scrambling Mina. From McKenzie's peripheral vision, she saw Cochran come out of the bushes. 'But wait,' her mind told her, 'Cochran is right behind Paxton.'

Cochran crashed into Jack who had moved out of the way of Paxton. Cochran, next to McKenzie stopped in mid stride when he recognizes himself tumbling now with Jack near the edge of the cliff. Rubi jumped to Mina and pulled her up to her feet, and they both turned to see Jack tumbling toward the cliff edge. McKenzie landed a hard kick to Paxton's shins and he fell to the ground hard. Cochran, in shock, watched himself fall with Jack over the cliff. Just as Jack disappeared from view he stretched his neck over Cochran and stained to see Mina. He mouthed "love" and then he was gone.

It took less than ten seconds as we measure time, but it was an infinite event Mina would attempt to process the rest of her life. The event didn't impact Cochran in the same personal way, but it shook him to the core.

McKenzie said, "I saw him, Mina. Something happened. It worked. I saw him."

Jacob bowed his head and quietly said to Rubi, "I should have been able to stop him. I was looking in the wrong direction."

"Jacob," Rubi said, 'it wasn't anybody's direct fault. The crazy man was after Mina. Jack just got in the way when that other man, who was trying to stop the loco guy, slammed into him. I did see it all, and I am still processing it. It's impossible, but I saw it."

"So you saw it too?" Jacob asked. "Did you see Mina's husband, Jack?"

"Yes," Rubi said. "He wasn't there, and then he was there."

"And the other guy that went over the cliff did you see him too?"

"Yes," Rubi said. "I saw the one chasing after the loco locomotive, but I saw him over by McKenzie too. I mean there were two of them."

"Right. That's what I saw too," Jacob said. He walked over to a still stunned Cochran and asked him, "Did you see your double just now?"

"It wasn't my double," Cochran said. "It was me." He walked over to the edge of the cliff and tried to see down the face of the mountain, but couldn't. The rock overhang shrouded the cliff and the jagged rocks 4,000 below. He felt a primal tug from the edge, but McKenzie was soon beside him, guiding him back to safety.

"Not your fault," McKenzie said quietly.

Cochran walked away without another word to anyone. Paxton pulled himself up to his feet and wobbled forward, following Cochran.

"You came with me?" Cochran asked.

Paxton looked at Cochran like he had two heads. "You pulled me along on your crazy caper. Between the wood splinters and that last kick, I am not sure my legs will ever be the same. Let's just get out of here. I don't know what just happened, and I don't care. There is no air left in my balloon.

Cochran grimaced and said, "Let's go home. You take the truck and follow me. I have another truck...," but when Paxton reached the spot where he had parked, there was no truck. Paxton cocked his head at Cochran again, shrugged his shoulders and walked to the truck Cochran was standing by just six parking spots away and got in.

Cochran hesitated, then turned off the ignition and got out, walking directly to Mina. "I don't know what just happened. I don't know if I caused that accident, but it was an accident. I don't even know if there were two deaths, just one or if anything real happened."

CHAPTER 19
JACK & MINA

WEDNESDAY
OCTOBER 7, 2015, 9:23 A.M.

"MYTH AND FANTASY ARE USUALLY based on the idea that where you fall, where you fail, where you find your greatest weakness, that is where you will also find your treasure," Mina told the rock she sat on. "Science says our future is determined by our past. God tells us our past only defines a starting point, not the end. But this feels like the end to me, not a starting point."

"It's a starting point, Mina," Jacob said, standing just behind her.

As Mina sucked in air sufficient to answer that ridiculous statement with a scream, she looked at Jacob's face that is smiling, ear-to-ear. Smiling and nodding at something. His smile disarmed her, and she turned to see what he is looking at. Jack was just pulling himself up from the edge of the cliff. As she had planned, but for an entirely different reason and mood, Mina let out a scream that for that moment subdued the breeze, increased the sunlight, and doubled the photosynthesis output in the trees around her.

Before she could stand, Jack dove to her. He embraced her as the prodigal son embraced his father. He was lost, and now he is found. He tried to speak, but no words came. Their tears mixed on each other's cheeks as they alternately held fast to each other and looked at each other's face. Finally, Jack spoke, "I was falling, and then I wasn't."

"I was falling, and now I'm not," Mina replied.

They sat, on their rock, holding each other and vowing to never let the other out of their sight. Rubi was the first to join them, adding her hugs and joy to theirs.

McKenzie nodded to Cochran who had turned from his walk back to his truck to see what caused the scream. He smiled at first because his police senses were tuned in like he was 35. He followed McKenzie's gaze to Mina and Jack just reaching out to embrace her. He paused for a minute or more to watch the happy reunion and also wondering if his other self was going to pull himself up over the cliff edge. He looked at McKenzie, doffed an imaginary hat, turned and walked back to his truck with a lighter step.

Jacob had initially backed away to make way for Jack to join Mina. The momentum of moving back took a surprising hold on him, and he just kept moving. Before he knew what he was doing, he was at Cochran's truck asking for a ride to the Fresno Airport.

"How did the truck driver find you?" Jack asked Mina minutes later.

"What truck driver?" Mina asked.

"I saw him standing by you as I pulled myself up from the cliff edge," Jack explained. "He's the guy who gave me a ride to California when Cochran left me in the forest."

"What forest?" Mina asked, suddenly realizing they both had some stories to tell each other.

"Later," Jack said, kissing Mina. "I just wanted to thank him. He was so selfless and had some wisdom to share that has meant a lot to me."

"That was Jacob," Mina said. She added when Jack still looked puzzled, "Jacob, as in Jacob's Gas Station." As Mina watched the light go on in Jack's understanding, she said, "He was my salvation at the San Francisco Library."

"He got me here too," McKenzie said. "He had just returned from California when I asked him to come back here with me. I knew I couldn't make the drive by myself and probably wouldn't be able to find you without his help."

"He is the person who called me to warn you about the danger of the crazy policeman," Rubi said. "I told you he was cute from his voice, right Mina? Admit it, am I good or what?"

"It appears we all owe him a great deal of gratitude," Jack said.

"We know where he lives," McKenzie said.

"I don't, but I want to," Rubi said. "I called him Jacob the Splitter yesterday. I didn't mean to hurt his feelings, but I think I must have. I was thinking out loud that it was at his gas station that both McKenzie's husband and you Jack, or you Mina, got split off from the same flow, or universe, or whatever the formal explanation is."

"Maybe he was," McKenzie said. "Him and his uncle who owned the station before him."

"That's just it," Rubi said. "I was standing right next to him today, and I saw what actually happened."

"What are you talking about?" Mina asked.

"Jacob was watching the trail. He had his back turned from you Mina," Rubi began. He turned around when that Paxton guy lost it. He turned around, and you appeared Jack. Everyone else already had eyes on the scene. Jacob is the observer, you know, of the cat in that experiment you told me about yesterday, McKenzie. He looked, and two paths became one. And more so, we now know, Schrödinger's cat is not dead, it's alive." Rubi smiled and looked from Mina to Jack.

"Jacob said it on the drive here," McKenzie said. "We are not bound by our past. Hope, faith, and love create our future."

"Jacob told me yesterday, something you taught him McKenzie. He said, "We don't see gravity, just its effect; its postmortem." Maybe the same is true for love. Love is a gift. It might even be a substance, but it is only rarely seen. Its effects, however, are everywhere. Its postmortem is our life.

"Jacob the Joiner," Jack said.

"I think he would prefer to be Jacob the Observer," McKenzie said. "He observes in both seeing, and doing."

"Someone needs to get him to observe the sorry state of his bathroom at his gas station," Jack said.

"I think he would prefer to not have a nickname and remain anonymous," Rubi said. "And I know just the person to get his gas station cleaned up."

"Count me out," Mina said. "I owe Jacob, but I get so scared thinking of walking into that gas station, I can't breathe. I'm still not convinced any of us really know what happened, or how we are now back together. For all I know, I will wake up soon, and it never happened, or that this reunion is a dream and we are still apart."

"And I'm not sure I ever want to run into Cochran again," Jack said. "The guy almost killed me, twice."

"Or you could say he gave his life for you," McKenzie said. "The Cochran that rolled over the cliff with you never came back."

"Or maybe Jacob the Observer saw Cochran, in effect, chose which Cochran would stay and the other disappeared," Rubi said. "If that iteration of Cochran disappeared, then it hardly could have slammed into you and rolled with you off the cliff. You are standing here today because Jacob chose wisely."

"And maybe he is standing here today," Mina said, "because I chose him over me and he chose me over him, and our love gave him the wings to not only come back up that cliff but cross the chasm between universes."

"So, what's the plan now?" McKenzie asked. "I for one have some goats and chickens to get back to."

"Can you give me a ride back to my place McKenzie?" Rubi asked. "Mina, I would plead for you to hang around, but I just said goodbye to you a couple weeks ago. I know you need to get on with your lives."

"Of course you can have a ride," McKenzie said. "In fact, you can have a ride to a great trout stream I know about. I hear you like to fish."

"Let's talk about that on the way to my place," Rubi said.

"And you two love birds?" McKenzie asked. "Continue your trip to Minnesota?"

"That ship has already sailed," Jack said.

"You once explained to me your theory of intersecting universes on a line from Minneapolis to San Francisco, right McKenzie?" Mina asked.

"That's my theory," McKenzie said.

"Then I want to be as far away from that line as possible," Mina said. You can come visit us in Florida this next winter McKenzie."

"Or Dublin," Jack said. "Didn't Twitter offer you a place in the Dublin office to try to keep you when you put in your notice? Like the wonderful person you are, you opted to follow me to Minneapolis. Maybe I should follow you to the Emerald Isle."

"My mother gave me my name to remind me of my Gaelic roots," McKenzie said. "I have never been to Scotland, and you would be just across the water. *Failte Alba*, We will survive my mother used to say. Applicable for the previous weeks we've experienced. Keep me up to date, whatever you decide. Come on Rubi, we're burning daylight."

Hugs were exchanged, and Mina and Jack watched the ladies leave. Then it was just them, alone, even though tourists now swarmed their rock.

"What do you want to do, Mina?" Jack asked as they sat back down.

"I have another night at Tenaya Lodge," Mina said. "Let's decide tomorrow. We should probably visit our parents. My mom is probably freaking out. I don't know what to tell them, though."

"My mom already had this thing semi-figured out as I tried to explain it to her," Jack said. Maybe by now, she can explain it to us. Let's just tell people the truth. While passing through Wyoming, we had a change of heart and a change of direction in our lives. We can tell them the rest after we figure it out."

"Do they have Cheetos in Ireland?" Mina asked.

CHAPTER 20
JACOB & JACOB & RUBI

Jacob landed in Laramie, Wyoming exhausted. All considered it was a miracle he was able to get back in the same day he showed up at the airport. Cochran dropped him off at the Fresno Airport at one in the afternoon. He was able to buy a seat to Denver that was scheduled to leave three hours later. He called the Tenaya Lodge to clear up his room and bought a $5 pastry at Starbucks. The hotel earned him a smile and a promise of a return trip when they said they wouldn't charge him for that night. He knew they couldn't use the room for another paying customer, and it was his fault for the late checkout, but they did it anyway. The flight left an hour late, but that still gave him two hours in Denver; plenty of time to get something to eat, stretch his legs, and call the rental car agency in Laramie so he could get home. It was less than an hour flight up to Laramie. He picked up his rental car with the plan to return it the next day after he found someone to pick him up at the airport and take him back to the gas station where he had left his truck. That was one of the problems with not having any friends. "But if Mina and Jack have taught me anything, it's that we don't have friends for what they can do for us. It's what we can do for them," he told the dashboard as he drove out of the airport.

Counting the rental car, the lavish dinner of a burger and fries in the Denver Airport, the two flights, half the diesel for McKenzie's fuel guzzling pickup truck, the hotel and food in California, "including the meals McKenzie volunteered me to cover," he spoke out loud with a smile, that trip had cost him just over a thousand dollars. "Then there was the previous roundtrip to California and the wages of his employee. "Wow, this breaking out of my shell stuff can get expensive."

Jacob immediately berated himself. "No counting costs," he reprimanded himself. "Let's count all the good things that have happened over the past week." He was still counting when he pulled into his home forty minutes later. His cabin felt even more empty than usual. Part of that might be that Beau was with his employee. He knew it was more than that. He had just spent more time, in close quarters, with more people than his black book held of all his Laramie friends, which was zero. He was asleep fifteen minutes later. He slept soundly until four the next morning. He tried to fall back asleep, but he was wide awake. He eventually accepted reality, got up, showered, ate a light breakfast of toast, an egg, and a small glass of orange juice. He really needed to do some grocery shopping. He drove to the gas station and parked there, looking at the gas pumps and the small building with different eyes. It was dark and quiet. It didn't look like the doorway to another universe, another reality, but apparently, it was.

He pulled out the tattered Bible he carried in the glove box of his truck that was still parked beside the station. He turned to a scripture he had been thinking a lot about lately. He read, "I returned, and saw under the sun, that the race is not to the swift, nor the battle to the strong, neither yet bread to the wise, nor yet riches to men of understanding, nor yet favor to men of skill; but time and chance happeneth to them all."

"I've returned, and I can attest to the fact that time and chance happeneth to us all," he said. "But uncertainties are best dealt with by the swift, the strong, and the wise. No that's not right," he corrected himself. Uncertainties are best dealt with by faith. The swift, the strong, the wise, might find some success in worldly ways, but when it comes to the real battle, give me the peaceable walker, the weak that can be made strong, and the unlearned that they may be taught."

He was thinking about himself with these words, but his mind soon drifted to Cochran—at first swift and strong, but as of yesterday, weak and teachable. "And seeing his own double? Then seeing his other self tumble off a cliff thousands of feet from the valley floor? Did his double share his knowledge before he died or disappeared? Surely as we go through life's experiences, those experiences go through us. They inform us. They change us. But do they change time? If they don't change time, then wouldn't it be great if we all had a double. We could live life twice, in parallel. Or a hundred times in parallel. A billion. We would all be living, breathing quantum computers."

McKenzie, first the wise teacher, then the humble student, talked about time on their drive to California. "Time is biological, managed by the brain," she had explained. "It's a perception, and we can change perception." Jacob got back out of his truck and locked it.

"Just because it's something we all rationally agree upon, doesn't mean it's there. Time helps us make sense of our existence, but so did Newtonian physics, until Einstein came along. And maybe someday quantum computers will prove him wrong." He wanted to open the store and try to return to his old life, but didn't have a set of keys with him, neither the physical ones nor the emotional ones. He got back into the rental car and drove to Laramie for a second breakfast while he waited for Ridley's Family Market to open.

After dropping off the fresh groceries at his cabin, Jacob drove back to the gas station. It was open for business. He was glad to see Ted, his only employee, was still working for him. "Hi, Ted," Jacob said like he had just stepped out for a few minutes.

"You're back," Ted said with a mix of surprise and exasperation. "I hope you don't plan on leaving again tonight or tomorrow."

"Now that you mention it," Jacob said, "I am leaving again." He waited a moment and then added, "I need you to follow me back to the airport so I can drop off this rental. Then you can have the rest of the day off, with pay. Thanks for all you have done to keep things going. It's been a crazy week, but that's the past now. Things are back to normal."

"Deal," Ted said. "I've got a girl to try to win back."

"By all means," Jacob said, "don't let her slip away."

"You're lucky you don't have a girlfriend to worry about Jacob," Ted said. "They are nothing but trouble."

"You're wrong, Ted," Jacob said, suddenly serious. "Love is powerful, and I am not talking about trading spit in the back seat of a car. You won't believe me, but that is a time waster."

"Speak for yourself, Jacob," Ted said grinning.

"I'm not saying it isn't fun," Jacob said. "But did you ever sit down to a video game or social media for say half an hour, and that led to an hour? That's a time waster. And wasting time is a sad excuse for life. What is your girlfriend's favorite book? What are her goals? What are her fears? Does she have any hobbies? Does she have someone she really respects? Why? Those are questions, and there are plenty more like them that never get answered because your mouth is otherwise occupied. And that occupation leads to other problems that are worse than time wasters."

"Thanks for the advice padre," Ted said.

"Take it or leave it," Jacob said, 'but I promise you that what I said will impact your life for good or bad, depending on how you follow through."

They left for the airport in separate vehicles and didn't talk much on the drive back to the gas station. As Jacob pulled off the Interstate, he said, "Hey Ted, sorry for coming on like that. Just something I have been thinking about lately, and I really do care about you. How about taking your girlfriend to dinner tonight on me? Ask her about her, and you just listen, really listen." He handed Ted two twentys, and Ted didn't utter a single word of complaint.

They pulled into the gas station, and there was a truck parked alongside the store. "Another customer that doesn't want to drive to Laramie for gas," Ted said. "Isn't that McKenzie's truck?" he asked as they pulled up alongside to park.

It was McKenzie's truck. Jacob did a quick calculation in his head. It had only been twenty-three hours since he had been standing beside her at Glacier Point. "She had to have driven almost straight through. There is no way."

Ted walked back to the store and unlocked it. He entered to collect his personal things, before leaving. Jacob walked over to McKenzie's truck. She was sitting there but was fast asleep. Jacob was about to knock on the window when he heard something behind him.

"So this is your kingdom?" Rubi asked as she turned the corner from behind the station.

Trying to hide his surprise, Jacob said, "No, this just finances the kingdom."

They looked at each other, not sure who should say something next. Jacob was the first to break the silence. "You drove straight through? You must be exhausted."

"It was McKenzie," Rubi said. "She talked me into spending a few days at her place. Something about some great fishing. Once we got started, she said she was worried about her goats."

"She's always got a plan, and stay out of her way when it comes time to execute, Jacob said. "Should we let her sleep while I show you around?"

"Sure," Rubi said.

"How about a bottle of orange juice on the house?" Jacob asked.

"How can a girl pass that up?" Rubi said as they walked to the store front door.

Jacob held the door, and Rubi entered. Ted was just about to leave and froze. "This is Ted," Jacob said. "My best employee."

"Yes," Rubi said. "I think we've met, on the phone. I have this kind of sixth sense about talking to a person on the phone and knowing what they look like. Great to meet you in person, Ted."

Ted offered his hand and suddenly realized it was clammy. He wiped it on his pants and then shook Rubi's hand. "You're the girl on the phone?" Ted asked.

"Yep, it's me," Rubi said.

"Ted was just leaving," Jacob said. "He has a hot date."

Ted walked to the door while Rubi walked to the drinks section along the back wall. When he passed Jacob, he whispered, "Talk about a hot date. You didn't say you had a friend who was Miss Universe." Jacob pushed him out the door and closed it.

"I was thinking on the way here Jacob," Rubi began as she opened her drink, "you and I have a lot in common. We both like fly fishing, and we are two of just a few people who have seen someone's double."

"It's only been a day, and I am already questioning my memories," Jacob said.

"About the double, or about me?" Rubi asked.

"I don't even know what to think about you," Jacob admitted.

"So, I got an advanced course in multiverses and gravitational waves from McKenzie last night. According to her," Rubi said, completely avoiding his answer, "science has supposedly proved Einstein's theory that gravitational waves bend time. Are we living witnesses that time can be completely bent, to the point that a person can be in two places at once until observed?"

"Quantum uncertainty exists, according to me," he said with a brief smile, "because we are uncertain beings. Uncertain who we are, where we are, why we are here, where we are going. You know, the standard meaning of life questions."

"So, if we are certain," Rubi asked, "how did we see?"

Jacob interrupted and asked, "Who says we are so certain?"

"I'm not," Rubi said. "But I know what I saw, and I know what happened. Basically, nothing happened until you turned and saw. Jacob, you were the observer that made it all happen. For scientists out there," she said as she waved her hand at the world outside the store, "the world of the atom is different than the world of people. An atom can be in two places at once until observed, but not your truck, not you."

"Observation might mean many things, Rubi," Jacob said. "A camera, a particle detector, or a human being. And on top of that, it's not like I see a world where the Vatican City won the World Cup Soccer Championship, or where Elvis became president. I don't see all the options. I just see what is in front of me, just like you."

"Maybe another thing we have both seen—Elvis's hair has come back to be president."

"Never thought of that," Jacob said, smiling again. "I do observe. Next to fishing, it's my favorite pastime. Lately, I have tried to fully observe—that is both see and then do. That new goal took me to California twice in one week. That new goal allowed me to observe you. It's love that is the power, not me."

"Hurray for your new goal," Rubi said with her own smile. "But that's why I think you have been the observer in all this. Those two atoms that are one atom when observed, don't communicate with each other. They act separate and autonomous, even though they have the same past. They don't sense the world around them in exactly the same way. That is until they reunite. You have been Jacob the Splitter, and now you are Jacob the Joiner. You said your Uncle mentioned a secret. Could that be it?"

"It's love that does the joining, Rubi," Jacob said. "Love that leads to selfless faith.

"How about love that leads to a kiss?" Rubi asked in a quieter voice.

"Is there such a thing as a selfless kiss?" Jacob asked approaching Rubi.

"There's no place for personal desire or personal need?" Rubi asked. "And for that matter, no place for curiosity, trial and error, emotional decisions? Being human?"

"Imperfection is the grist that shines the rock," Jacob said.

"It's more than that," Rubi said. "It's the crack that lets the light in, it's the hope that lets us all know we haven't arrived, but all is not lost. Not being perfect allows us to try, to test, to leap, to fail, and then get up again. And dear Jacob, imperfection leads to change and discovery. You are living proof."

"But knowing that "perfect" exists," Jacob said, "is the engine that keeps this imperfect system running. If imperfection were the end game, there would be nothing on your list. We try, we fail, we try, we die. I'm not talking about those instances of temporary or perceived perfection; that perfect day, playing a musical piece without a wrong note, your checkbook balancing to the penny, or achieving a goal without even one failure for a whole day or week. I am talking about all of us not having to compare ourselves to each other because there is something so perfect that our horizontal similarities fade away into unimportance because of the majesty of the vertical comparison. That's what makes selfless love possible."

"You lost me after "It's love that does the joining, Rubi," Rubi said. "Not really, but let's get back to that subject."

Neither realized they were holding each other's hands and that their faces were only inches apart. That realization struck them both at the same time. They blushed and spoke simultaneously. They both leaned into each other to kiss when they heard a noise outside. Someone had tossed a small pebble at the window. Jacob turned, expecting to see McKenzie.

Both caught their breath. Just outside the window was a double of Jacob. The double smiled, nodded his head, and disappeared. They went outside, and no one was there. Literally, no one was there. McKenzie must have woken up and left.

CHAPTER 21
COCHRAN

FRIDAY
OCTOBER 9, 2015, 2:29 P.M.

COCHRAN TOOK TWO DAYS TO drive home. In that time he hardly talked with Paxton. He wasn't rude, but he wasn't overly friendly either. He felt mostly responsible that he had pulled Paxton into this crazy scheme in the first place. As the miles rolled by, he came to realize his pursuit of the Gambles was more about his problems than their crazy stories, which he had manufactured into something even crazier. He had made some terrible threats and almost gotten people seriously hurt. "There are three kinds of crazy," his training officer had told him many years ago. "When someone believes something that isn't true, and you just can't help them see reality. That's all those conspiracy crazies. "Airline contrails are really the government poisoning us." You can ask those people why the government is wasting so much poison over Wyoming where there aren't any people, but they are still going to go on believing their myth. Second, there are those crazies that reject the truth when it is staring them in the face. Finally, there are those, from either of the first two groups who keep doing the same thing and expect a different outcome." Cochran knew he had been an enthusiastic participant on both sides of that coin and its edge.

He actually suppressed a smile as he pulled into the car port alongside his trailer. "Home sweet home," he said as he unlocked the front door. The place was a mess and he honestly couldn't remember leaving it that way. "Chaos just is," he said, echoing some of the sites he found online when he was obsessed with time travel. "That is just a theory of a bunch of people who think they are smarter than they are, but actually can't see beyond their nose. Who says that chaos is just so complex we can't understand it? Who says miracles, for that matter, don't also follow some rules beyond our grasp? I saw something in the California mountains. Whatever I saw, it was beyond simple crazy and beyond randomness. There is more to who and what we are and where and how we live. So I am sick and tired of my life and this dump I live in? Instead of finding an excuse, how about I face my life and change it myself?"

Cochran still had two days left on his scheduled vacation. He had his home cleaned up by noon the next day. Calling his office to let them know he would be in on Monday, he received some interesting news. He tucked that away to stay focused in the big challenge of the day. He called his ex-wife after finishing lunch.

"Hey Katy, it's me," he began.

"Do you need money? Because I don't have any to bail you out of whatever corner you've painted yourself into this time," she said.

"No, no problems," he said, not getting upset like he usually did. "Just calling to say sorry."

"For what? Are you drunk?" she asked.

"Nothing in particular, and pretty much everything," he said with a chuckle. "And no, I'm not drunk. I took a little time off and didn't touch any alcohol. Didn't have time to actually.

Anyway, I've had time to think and I know I really blew it with us. I'm not calling to try to get back together, just trying to take a few steps the right direction."

"And what direction is that?" she asked, still sounding skeptical.

"Still trying to sort through that too," he said. "The kind of direction where I don't create all those bad or bad, either or options so no matter what I choose I know I will lose and it won't be my fault. I know there are other options now. Millions of other options."

"I have talked to you about that hundreds of times," she said. "Faulty dilemmas, remember? You laughed in my face. What's got you thinking so straight?"

"Not sure I'm really thinking straight yet," he said. "Let's just say I had the opportunity to watch myself fall over a cliff and I lived to tell about it."

"A vision of the future and you didn't like it?" She said. "I'm glad, really glad."

"Sort of traveling to the future that is actually in the past, all rolled up in the present," he said. "Mostly I feel better than I have in years and I want to be done with a life where I spend so much energy trying to avoid choices I need to make because I am afraid of the accountability that comes with those choices. I think I am relearning that responsibility is where freedom lives. Trying to avoid duty, does not let me escape culpability. So that's why I thought I would call and say I'm sorry."

"Wow, Cochran," she said after a silent pause. "I haven't heard you talk like this in years."

"I haven't felt like this in years," he said. "Anyway, I don't want to take up your day. I've got some laundry and dirty dishes calling my name. I start back to work day after tomorrow."

"I apologize too," his ex said.

"Now I am really lost," Cochran said. "What do you have to apologize for?"

"Entropy," she said.

"Huh?" he mumbled.

"Ever since I left you I have believed that your life was nothing but a gradual decline into disorder," she explained. "Someone told me that was a definition of entropy. Just sounds more scientific and official, like a stamp on the paper explaining your life. So I've created my own faulty perspectives."

"Well, I have certainly earned the title," Cochran said with a lighthearted tone in his voice. "Maybe there is local entropy, even if at the same time the universe is still expanding. New worlds are created and I still have dirty dishes from two weeks ago."

"Now I'm lost," his ex said.

"Just some things I have been researching and thinking about," Cochran said. "There are things I wish I had done differently in my life. I wish time travel were possible, so I could do them better. In order to travel back in time, space would have to decrease, not just get compressed. Even black holes just compress space. They might vacuum up stars, but space just gets crushed, not destroyed."

"I'm still lost Cochran," his ex said, "and you aren't doing a very good job proving to me you aren't drunk, but here's the thing babe, you don't have to travel back in time to undo and start over. Today is the starting point for the rest of your life. Your past is not a prison where you lock up your criminal behavior. Your past is a school of hard knocks and some amazing blessings. Learn from your mistakes and don't let them demand more of you. You might need to work some things out with God, but He's on your team too."

"Too?" Cochran asked. "Who else is on my team?"

"Me, you dummy," she said. "I'm not saying that because I want to get back together either, but I am your friend. Last I looked maybe your only true friend. Those drunks you hang out with aren't your friends, that's for sure. Sorry, there I go again making judgments about people."

"I met some interesting people the other day," he said. "And apology accepted. I earned all your negative feelings about me. I hope I can earn the kindness of your present hopefulness about my future. I better go though. I am taking up way too much of your time."

"I wouldn't want to be the one to stand in the way of those dirty dishes," she said. "Here's an idea. You said you had another day of vacation. Why not stop by tomorrow for lunch. Cheyenne is only an hour away."

"I have a couple errands to take care of in the morning. If that works out, I will call and confirm that offer for lunch."

The dishes were done, the laundry in the dryer, and Cochran decided to take care of one errand yet today. He drove out to Jacob's gas station. He pulled in and filled his tank. He walked into the store and was surprised to see that other girl, from California, talking with Jacob.

"Hey Jacob, mam" Cochran said as he nodded to them both. "Any free donuts today?"

Jacob would not be disturbed by Cochran's attitude today. He smiled and tossed Cochran a box of Hostess Cup Cakes.

"Thanks, Jacob," Cochran said. "You owe me more than this box," he added in an official tone. He noticed the girl, 'what was her name?', trying to throw darts with her eyes at him. He smiled and added, "You owe me contempt, anger, frustration, revenge, hurt, sadness, and probably your fist against my nose. Instead, you offer me this box of cupcakes. So thank you, Jacob. I came here to apologize and maybe take a step toward friendship. I thought you and I were similar in that neither of us had any real friends. I see you are far ahead of me in that department. But I hope, ever time, we can become friends." He put a hundred dollar bill on the counter and walked out the door.

After making a few calls the evening before, Cochran showed up early at McKenzie's place, followed by another man in his own truck. McKenzie came out of her barn wondering what all the racket was. When she saw Cochran, she grunted, realizing he was between her and her shotgun inside the house. He had brought someone else with him. McKenzie didn't know him. She absentmindedly rubbed the side of her face where she had been hit recently.

McKenzie's hand on her face did not go unnoticed by Cochran. It was like he had just been hit in the gut.

"What is it you want, Cochran?" McKenzie said as she walked toward her house, hoping she could get by him without being knocked to the ground again.

"Not so fast McKenzie," Cochran said. "I don't want to talk to you with your shotgun pointing at me."

"I'll bet you don't, you balled up cobweb," McKenzie said.

The man with Cochran chuckled and then looked at the ground.

"I deserve much worse than that," Cochran said. "This is Smitty. He is the best carpenter in town. He is here for two reasons. First, he is here to fix your porch. Second, he is here as a witness. If you want to press charges against me, and I wouldn't blame you if you did. In fact, if I were you I would. Smitty is here to witness this and will support you in court. Paxton should not be counted on to tell the truth because he would get into trouble too."

"What's your game, Cochran," McKenzie asked.

"No game, but I am here to apologize for everything," Cochran said. "I know that apology would sound pretty hollow coming from me, so I brought Smitty and his talents as back up."

McKenzie just stared at Cochran, trying to discern whether he was being honest or if this was some other twisted way to get her to explain time travel to him.

"I also owe you for the drive you took to California," Cochran continued. "I figure you wouldn't have gone except out of fear for me and Paxton. I don't know how much that cost and you probably had someone here to watch your animals while gone. I figure $500 might cover that. I don't have that much money right now, but I will make installment payments."

McKenzie was still silent, but her face didn't look as hard as it did when she first recognized him

"I take that as an enthusiastic agreement to my terms," Cochran said. "Would you like me to put my attacks against you in writing because I did that this morning?" Cochran pulled out several folded sheets of paper from his jacket pocket and tried to hand them to her.

"You can take your written confession and," McKenzie paused, took a breath and said, "You know what you can do? You can fold them up and put them under the porch floorboards that I will allow you to replace. As for the money; you don't owe me a dime. I wouldn't have missed that for the world."

"Me neither," Cochran said. "You might say it was my death and resurrection."

"Pardon me if I don't stand too close," McKenzie said. "Talk like that, and you are going to get hit by lightning."

"No claims of wisdom, or any special status, certainly I'm not deity," Cochran said. "Maybe closer to the other side, or underside, of that status. But you got to admit, that you saw what I saw. The rest is up to me."

"I saw," McKenzie said. "I've always known you had some good in you. Don't forget I know you when you still needed to be burped as a brand new cop."

"I don't expect trust to happen overnight," Cochran continued, "but I want to earn it back, even if it takes another twenty-five years. Now if it's alright, I have another appointment in Cheyenne at noon, so I need to be going. Smitty will send me the bill, so make sure you get exactly what you want with those porch repairs."

"Before you go, since you are looking for resurrection of a sort," McKenzie said. "You need to go straighten things out with Jacob. My injuries were mostly physical and those repair. His are of a deeper sort. And they were rubbed in with the salt of no thought like he didn't even exist."

"I know," Cochran said, tears brimming in his eyes. "I went to visit with him last night. I don't deserve the forgiveness of either of you, and I know it will take years and my own actions, not just my absence to make it up. That girl was at the station with him. Are they?"

"Just friends right now," McKenzie said. "She is staying with me. Jacob brought her by late last night. I heard her come in, but I was already in bed. She left this morning with him to go fishing. She didn't mention your visit."

"Just as well," Cochran said. "I am not looking for notoriety, just trusted anonymity. I doubt I will ever be a friend. And what about the Gambles, Mina and Jack? Are they going to be back this way anytime soon? I have some information for them."

"And what might that be?" McKenzie asked, on guard once again.

"Their car," Cochran said. "The Cheyenne Police found it. Totaled. I hate to pass on the bad news."

"After what you've been passing on," McKenzie said with a laugh, "I am sure this won't even phase them. So their car really was stolen. That might actually be good news for them."

"As I think about it," Cochran said, "I think I will let the Cheyenne police make that call. I don't want to cause any PTSD. Tell them I wish my best, whatever that might be."

"Your best is quite a bit Officer Cochran, now get going. I still have goats to milk."

CHAPTER 22
FRANK & McKENZIE

GOATS MILKED FOR THE SECOND time that day, animals fed and bedded down for the night, McKenzie felt good. She hesitated, however, to enter the house. She paused at the top of the porch steps and admired the carpentry work Smitty had done. Cochran's visit was a surprise, but his change of heart and attitude were not. Secretly, McKenzie had felt sorry for the downward spiral Cochran's life seemed to be in over the last ten years. Once he hit bottom, she believed he was strong enough to start the upward climb. She felt good about this turnaround. Not just for Cochran, but what it said about humanity. Everyone should get a second chance. Even her? Maybe not.

She knew she didn't want to go inside the house. It was empty. Just like her heart. This feeling came over her at the end of most every day, even in bad weather. And like every day of the past two decades she gritted her teeth and went inside. An hour later she was washed up, had eaten dinner, and looked forward to an early night, as she was still catching up on her sleep. Just as she was starting to read the August edition of *Ranch & Rural Living Magazine* her cell phone rang.

"Hello," she said, knowing it was Rubi.

"McKenzie, I hate to bother you, and if you can't it's fine, but can you come and pick me up at the gas station?" Rubi said, bubbling over with enthusiasm.

"Sounds like it was a good day for fishing," McKenzie said.

"We caught a few, well, Jacob caught a few. I'm not in his league, yet," Rubi said. "He really needs to stay at the store. His employee Ted has a hot date, or something, and Jacob said he would take me home, but he also feels like he needs to let Ted take some time off."

"Relax, I'm on my way," McKenzie said. She was happy to get out of the house and to actually get to see Rubi and Jacob. The sun hadn't hit the horizon yet, and it was a peaceful evening. Even the bugs seemed to be taking the evening off. Usually, by the time she arrived at the gas station this time of day and year, she had to spend the first five minutes scraping bugs off her windshield.

She was surprised that Jacob and Rubi weren't there. She went inside and the young man that Rubi had called Ted, explained that they were on their way. McKenzie went back outside to fill up her truck since she was waiting. "Never leave the gas station except with a full tank," Frank used to say.

The gas nozzle had just clicked off with a full tank when Jacob and Rubi pulled up. Jacob also pulled his truck up to the other side of the same pump to fill up. He got out and turned to look at the store to confirm Ted was still there. Instead of Ted walking out to leave for his date, another young man exited. He was older than Ted, and his clothes were slightly odd. Jacob couldn't put his finger on what was different. Rubi walked around to McKenzie's truck, thinking nothing of the man exiting the store.

"Hey McKenzie," Rubi said. "Thank you so much for coming out here."

McKenzie walked to the back of her truck to give Rubi a hug. Jacob's truck had been blocking the view of the store from McKenzie. When she turned to greet Rubi, she caught her breath. Her hand came to her mouth and she froze.

"You okay?" Rubi asked. "It looks like you just saw a ghost."

"I did, I mean I do," McKenzie sputtered.

Rubi turned and looked in the direction of McKenzie's ghost. She saw a young man walking toward them. He looked different. Rubi realized the cut of his jeans were old fashioned looking, or maybe that was some new fashion. His shirt was a thick flannel with the sleeves rolled up. His short hair was simple. For some reason, Rubi felt like she was looking at an old magazine. 'How amazing,' she thought, 'that our eyes can pick up such minute detail and our brains have a hard time sorting it out.'

"Frank?" McKenzie called, her voice barely audible to Rubi who was right next to her.

Frank smiled and waved at her.

"Frank?" Rubi asked McKenzie. "You mean your husband, Frank? That young man is your husband?"

"That's what he was wearing when he went into the station over twenty years ago," McKenzie said. "I look horrible, and I am an old woman. He can't see me like this." She tried to hide behind Rubi.

"Jacob walked over to Frank before he reached McKenzie and Rubi. "Hi, I'm Jacob. I own this station. Can I help you?"

"You're the Bridgemaster?" Frank asked.

"The what?" Jacob asked.

"The Bridgemaster. The previous owner was the Bridgemaster. He passed away I take it," Frank said.

"Yes, seven years ago," Jacob explained. "He was my uncle."

"Oh, I'm sorry. And, I am sure he is grateful you found your gift," Frank said. I knew your Uncle where I just came from. He was a good and kind man. He loved everyone who visited this station. So is that McKenzie?"

Jacob wanted to ask more about this Bridgemaster thing, and the uncle he had barely known, but said, "That's her, but an older her or you're a younger you," feeling like he was in a dream; both excited and worried for McKenzie.

"I understand, and don't worry," Frank said. "I think things are going to work out. Let's go talk with her. It would be good for you to hear this."

Frank walked over to McKenzie and smiled while tears ran down his cheeks. McKenzie was also crying. Frank, who originally appeared to be in control was at a loss for words. McKenzie finally said, "If I had known you would be here, I would have worn nicer clothes, maybe put on some makeup."

"Those are the eyes I remember," Frank said. "You haven't changed a bit. I want you to come home with me." Frank could feel McKenzie's hands tense up.

"This is home, Frank," McKenzie said.

"Home can be wherever we can be together, Kenz," Frank said. "We have lost too many years apart. What if I told you we can have them back and spend them together?"

"I would say you are nuts," McKenzie said. "But then I see how old you are and, well, I'm listening. But before you say anything, I want you to know I love you, I love you, and I love you."

"I know you do, Kenz," Franks said. "I wouldn't be able to be here if you didn't." He looked at the small group of McKenzie, Jacob, and Rubi. "I don't know how much time I have here and I am guessing I am here for two reasons. One is to bring McKenzie back with me. The other is to share what understanding I have with the Bridgemaster, that's you, Jacob. Let's sit in the back of your truck Kenz. It's better than going back into the store."

They wordlessly agreed and jumped into the back of the truck, Jacob sitting with Rubi on the floor at the front of the truck bed and McKenzie and Frank sitting across from each other on each wheel well. It was apparent to all that McKenzie was still in shock and very uneasy about this young Frank and her weather worn older self.

"I hope the bugs don't eat us alive out here," Frank began, "but as you might have figured out, the store itself is the bridge. The other side is not one place but many places. They are just like here but differ slightly by the choices individuals make. It isn't every conceivable difference that science suggests because people have some predisposed notions, interests, and desires, and of course, the principles that decide outcomes are universal and never change. President Kennedy was still assassinated where I have been. President Nixon still resigned, and World War Two and Vietnam still happened."

"So the other universes are just direct copies of here?" Rubi asked. Both Jacob and McKenzie silently marveled that Rubi was taking to this unbelievable situation with little difficulty or hesitation.

"No, there are differences. Little choices add up to significant changes. The speed limit here in Wyoming is 55 miles per hour, for example. That might lead to fewer deaths, and one of those might be pivotal to some other event that a person who might have died here will play. On the other hand, a baby might not be born healthy because the mother didn't make it to the hospital in time. The interesting thing is, as far as I can tell, the multiverses have this balancing measure with each other. Not every person is in every reality. There was no McKenzie where I just came from. There was no Frank here, at least I am assuming that. But there is enough movement between realities that things are not that much different. That is, key moments in history as we know it, pretty much turn the same direction. Nuclear destruction didn't happen in another world because the guy that chose not to push the button here had a bad day there and launched Armageddon."

"So why is that?" Rubi continued. "Just some natural balance?"

"Yes, and no," Frank said. "Just before our last meeting, Kenze, I developed a theory, part of which I shared with you. We talk about the four forces of nature, but there is a fifth, Love."

"I shared that with these two and with a couple that got separated here at this gas station and were recently reunited," McKenzie said.

"Great, then you can follow my thought that love is a balancing force," Frank said.

"So love is a natural force that science here has not quite come to grips with?" Jacob asked.

"I don't think so," Frank said. "Remember, this is just my theory. I don't have all the answers, but I did get to talk with Jacob's Uncle and I have had more time to sort things out as best as I could. I still believe in God as the creator and author of worlds and the source of pure love—that fifth force. I don't know how religious you are, even you, Kenze. It's been quite a few years since we've talked."

"We have all come to our own sense that there is more to our lives than we are born, live, procreate, and die," McKenzie said. "I don't want to speak for each person's faith here, but I would say we are ready to hear your theory."

"Science is the big gamble, not religion," Frank said. "Don't get me wrong. Science has an important role to play in our lives. It offers options. It offers choices. It offers paths to discovery and even creation. But science is not in charge. It is a tool, not the master craftsman. We have all become novice craftsmen with this tool in our hands, and we have convinced ourselves we are the masters and that our tools are powerful. Yet, the more we find, the more we fail to see reality."

"So, I think I agree," McKenzie said. "I also know what I know. We were stuck in alternate universes, and it was science that explained it. Science that offered hope that I would get you back."

"Don't be so sure," Frank said, standing up and crossing the truck bed to kiss her forehead and then sitting back down next to her. "Just because we can't explain it; just because science claims to explain it with complexity that actually only hides the truth, doesn't mean it's unexplainable. There was an Oxford philosopher, Richard Swinburne. I don't know, maybe he is still alive. He brought up a valid point when he said, "It is crazy to postulate a trillion causally unconnected universes to explain the features of one universe when postulating one entity, God, will do the job.""

"Faith and science work best hand-in-hand, not opposed to each other," Jacob said more to himself than the group.

"I remember the other thought you shared in our last letter exchange," McKenzie said. "It was from Max Planck, who ironically is considered the father of Quantum Physics. He said something like, "Anybody who has been seriously engaged in scientific work of any kind realizes that over the entrance to the gates of the temple of science are written the words: Ye must have faith. It is a quality which the scientist cannot dispense with.""

"The miracle and the mundane, the spiritually divine and the spiritually destitute, the burning bush and the burning dumpster coexist in our world of choices," Jacob said, again more to himself than to the group.

"I can see why you are the Bridgemaster, Jacob," Frank said. "Your uncle would be very proud. It's because of your awakening understanding of the power and operation of love that I am here right now and that I can stay here for a short time. You already know this Jacob, but it's not about you. You, and your uncle before you, have been entrusted with the guardianship of a physical location where not only two realities intersect, but where love is sometimes tested and always strengthened. And yes, in some circumstances I can't explain, that strengthening begins with a split that demands a resolution. In those cases, you help unlock the door. You hold no special powers, but your assistance in seeing and doing is both a stewardship and a heavy responsibility. Who knows, there may be other intersections where two realities meet and a Bridgemaster stands guard there as well. What would have happened today if you would have decided to tear down this gas station, or simply sell it when you uncle passed away? I probably wouldn't be here. I don't understand it all, and I am the first to say maybe I've got it all wrong, but love and faith are a real part of my life, and it has taken me a long time to realize that I had to let you go Kenze, in order to have you. So let me complete my theory and then I need to go."

McKenzie took in an audible breath but didn't say anything.

"On the vast scale of universes, General Relativity does an amazingly accurate job of explaining reality. Gravitational waves play a role in the balancing between realities that I just mentioned, for example. Black holes destroy existence, there is position certainty, space is smooth but experiences gravitational stretching, and time is relative. On the minute scale, Quantum Mechanics does a great job. Time is constant, space is chopped up and bumpy, position is uncertain—the whole being in two places at once until being observed phenomena, and from this perspective, black holes do not destroy information. The depth behind these statements will have to wait for another meeting if one happens. In between these two theories is where we live. We aren't individual atoms, and we aren't universes. We are people. We seem to live in a Quantum Relativity. Just a theory. God knows the actual process."

"So the opposing rules of both theories apply?" Rubi asked.

"It's the zone where the fifth force of love has the strongest influence," Frank said. "From the point of view of Einstein's Theory of Special Relativity, Quantum Mechanics requires that information travel between points a and b faster than the speed of light. That is, if measurement "a" really affects what happens when "b" is made, observers from whom "b" happens first will see affect precede the cause. How can that be? Love, the Speed of Love, is instantaneous. Or if it could be measured, it's infinitesimally faster than the speed of light."

"And as humans," Jacob said, "created in the image of God the creator, we also create, in a sense, because of our ability to apply love. I mean, for any other part of reality, love is a force, not a tool. For humans, we can actually harness love."

"And as humans," Frank added, "we have the ability to forget, to reject the power of love, which may be another tool. Love and the choice to use it or not, are not independent of us. It comes so naturally to us that we use it or don't use it without much thought. There is a connection between our physical reality and our use or misuse of love. In most cases of human love, we create our own time lag. It's not love that moves slow, but us. The more we can selflessly love, the more powerful this tool becomes. The less bound by space and time we are. At one level of our development, we hold tight to the idea that "seeing is believing." As we grow in our understanding of this powerful gift, we can say with confidence that "believing is seeing." Faith is a product of our love, and faith allows us to apply love in powerful ways."

"You said love is a gift," Rubi interjected.

"Authentic love is given, not taken," Frank said. "There are no strings attached, no quid pro quo, no selfish motive, with love as I am describing it as a force of nature. And the author of love, Jesus Christ, gave it freely without requirement, without reciprocal conditional demands. Love isn't deserved, it's a gift. It's not a sales transaction where we exchange something to get love. Oh, we can believe we create love, barter love, exchange mutual self-benefit love, but that is just a clever counterfeit of real love. That kind of love is quantitative and measurable. That is one reason why science will want to reject the idea of love as a force. Love is actually immeasurable and qualitative. Real love disallows lasting conflict, deepens intimacy, and strengthens bonds between ourselves and the "other." Otherness, every individual, and living thing, from plants to animals, to groups we categorize as different than us in some way, is the object of our love. Certainly, we need to love ourselves—that is, to have a healthy care for our own wellbeing and to understand and revere who we are and what our potential is. That comes from within, but is nurtured by the love freely and unconditionally given by others."

"So where does that leave us?" McKenzie asked. Jacob wondered if she meant us as humans, or us as in the "Frank and McKenzie" us.

"That, my dear Kenz, is up to us," Frank answered, leaving the question of us up to McKenzie to decide.

"Why are you so young and McKenzie, so um, farther along in time?" Rubi asked.

"I honestly don't know," Frank said. "Maybe there is a time variance between realities, and this is how I look here, relative to there. I know if McKenzie comes with me," and he turned to look a McKenzie, "if you come back with me Kenz, you will be a younger you. Time is just a relative thing after all. With love, the end can fall somewhere before the beginning."

"And why can't you just stay here?" McKenzie asked. "Not that I don't want to go, but I just don't understand. Jack, from the other couple that was separated and was recently reunited, he was somewhere else, and he came back here."

"I don't know the answer to that either," Frank said. "I suppose it has to do with the balance of love in each place. I could probably come back from time to time, but I doubt I could wander too far away from here or stay too long. That's just a feeling, not a fact. But it's something I don't want to test without you by my side, Kenze."

"Okay, Frank," McKenzie said. Turning to Rubi, she said, "Can you take care of my place? I know you have a life and family in California, but there are animals to feed, goats to milk."

"And streams to fish, and a boy to pursue," Rubi interjected. "I was born for this, McKenzie. I have been a fish out of water for most of my life. I feel whole here. I can sort everything except explaining your disappearance. I don't want to be hauled in for your murder and taking over your place."

"I can sign over my place to you, and I think Cochran will help clear the road of any obstacles," McKenzie said. "And who knows, the better you get at pragmatation, well, who knows, maybe we'll come back for a visit now and then. Especially as Jacob here learns the ropes of being a Bridgemaster. You might really enjoy some of the anadexterous passages that happen at the gas station. No pressure Jacob, but I would like to see Mina and Jack again. Give them all my love, will you, in case I can't get back?"

"I will," Rubi said. "They will be thrilled to hear you have been reunited with Frank.

"I have a feeling that the more we are able to align our values, our desires, with the principles Frank has been talking about, the more our realities will become one," Jacob said.

"Maybe we are all Bridgemasters," Rubi said.

"Finders Weepers, Losers, Keepers," Frank said.

"*There is one who scatters,*" McKenzie said from memory, "*and yet increases all the more, And there is one who withholds what is justly due, and yet it results only in want. Psalms 11:24. FWLK, Frank Walker Louis Karas.*"

Frank helped McKenzie out of the truck bed. McKenzie pulled a pad of paper out of her glove box in the cab and wrote a note to Cochran and another signing over her ranch to Rubi. Jacob and Rubi followed Frank and McKenzie into the store.

McKenzie turned to Jacob and said, "For the sake of all humankind, Jacob, clean that bathroom. I am never going to come back if I have to go through that place ever again." She turned and took Frank's hand and as she opened the door to the bathroom, the years fell off her frame, and she looked like the young woman that lost her Frank over two decades ago. She turned and blew a kiss to Rubi and Jacob, and she and Frank held their noses as they closed the bathroom door behind them.

Rubi walked to the bathroom door, opened it and there was no one there. She smiled and walked back to Jacob. "Let's clean that bathroom and then, well, do you think the fish are biting?"

"Perfect day for some catch and release," Jacob said.

Additional works on sale by this author:
(recent works available at Amazon.com)

Transitions from Military Rule in South America: The Obligational Legitimacy Hypothesis
Published by Naval Postgraduate School Press, 1987,
210 pages; Approved for public release.

Long-term Success: A New Paradigm for Personal and Enterprise Achievement
Published by Byblos Press, June 2003; 40 pages;
ISBN 0-9746003-1-8

The Seeds He Planted
Published by Byblos Press, December 2007
ISBN 978-0-9746003-2-1

Nahum's Story
Published by Byblos Press, December 2007
ISBN 978-0-9746003-3-8

Media in the 21st Century: Meet-Up or Meltdown in the Meaning Marketplace
Published by Byblos Media, June 2010; 583 pages
ISBN 978-0-9746003-6-9

Conversations Among Butterflies
Published by Byblos Media, August 2015; 393 pages;
ISBN 978-0-9746003-7-6

Kitab Kabbani
Published by Byblos Media, November 2015; 407 pages;
ISBN 978-0-9746003-8-3

Chinese Circus
Published by Byblos Media, 2016, 437 pages;
ISBN13 978-0-9746003-9-0

Cambalache
Published by Byblos Media, 2017, 451 pages;
ISBN13 978-0-9990111-0-2

Upcoming Fiction and Non-Fiction works by this author:

see www.mike-mitchell.com

For more information:

www.mike-mitchell.com

Sign up for the author's mailing list at:

www.eepurl.com/bviacf

Or scan the QR code

www.ingramcontent.com/pod-product-compliance
Lightning Source LLC
Chambersburg PA
CBHW061229170626
46809CB00007B/2589